THE REFUGE

MONICA HUGHES
THE REFUGE

Stoddart

First published in softcover in 1992 by
Stoddart Publishing Co. Limited
34 Lesmill Road
Toronto, Canada
M3B 2T6

First published in hardcover in 1989 by
Doubleday Canada Limited

Published by arrangement with Doubleday Canada Limited

Canadian Cataloguing in Publication Data

Hughes, Monica, 1925–
The refuge

"Junior Gemini"
ISBN 0-7736-7737-6

I. Title

PS8565.U43R43 1992   jC813'.54   C92-095289-5
PZ7.H83Re 1992

Cover illustration: Brian Deines

Printed and bound in Canada

*Stoddart Publishing gratefully acknowledges the support of
the Canada Council, Ontario Ministry of Culture and
Communications, Ontario Arts Council and Ontario
Publishing Centre in the development of writing and
publishing in Canada.*

To my children,

who discovered and named

their "Campbell's Bush"

a long time ago

ONE

It began with the jackrabbit. Or perhaps three weeks earlier, when Barbara watched her bedroom furniture being carried out of the house and put into the moving van. She went back indoors and wandered through the echoing, empty rooms. Standing at the french windows in the dining room, she stared at the smooth lawn and the orderly flowerbeds that contrasted with the tangle of the ravine beyond.

Remembering. The smell of fresh coffee and bacon frying. The sound of their voices.

"Good morning, Dad."

"Morning, chicken."

"It's a glorious Saturday, Dad. Could we maybe . . . ?"

"Sorry. Not a chance. Too busy making money for your mother to spend." His light laugh, and Mom's voice, shaky with emotion, taking the bait. Why did she always fall for it? Dad was only funning, wasn't he?

"That's simply not fair, Larry. This house was your choice, not mine. The country club . . . good grief, what do *I* want with a country club?"

Barbara turned away from the window, her hands over her ears. *Stop it! Stop it!* . . . She blinked. There was no one there. The room was empty of everything but a shred of newspaper and a carton of china still to be picked up.

She walked slowly upstairs, running her hand lovingly along the curved banister. What would life be like away from the place that had been home for twelve years? But the voices were up here too, echoing from her parents' room. Only bickering, she had told herself. Everyone does it. Look at Mercedes and Suzanne. They never stopped. Surely it didn't have to end like *this*?

She looked out the upper hall window and saw Mercedes coming up the walk. She pounded gladly downstairs, leaving the voices and echoes behind.

"This is the worst day in my whole total life. To be leaving Willow Heights! I can't believe it. I just know I'll never see you again. Mercedes, isn't it totally the end?"

"You're only moving to the north side. It's not that far. And we can always phone each other, you know."

"I bet you'll forget all about me. Anyway, you'll be away for the next two months. Where are you going *this* year?"

Mercedes' dad was one of the richest in a neighbourhood of rich fathers.

"Mom and I are staying with relatives in Maine for a month. Then Dad's meeting us and we're going on a cruise somewhere or other. What about you?"

"We'll be stuck in the city for practically *two whole months.* Can you believe it? Nothing to do and nowhere to

2

go. I'm going to hate every single minute of it."

"Poor Barb. I'll send you postcards. And I'll phone as soon as I get back, I promise."

"Goodbye, Mercedes!" Barbara flung her arms around her friend.

The movers slammed and bolted the van doors and climbed up into the cab. Barbara's mother came out of the house and shut and locked the front door with a final sound. She hurried down the walk dangling the keys, her mousy hair ruffled and untidy, her expression harried.

"Into the car, Barb. We mustn't keep them waiting at the other end. Mercedes, will you give the keys to your mother, please? The agent will pick them up later today. Goodbye, dear."

Her mother pushed Barb into the car, among the suitcases and the precious bundles that she didn't trust to the movers. Barb struggled to turn around for a last look at the house. It had been described in the *Real Estate Weekly* as "a two-storey mansion finished in grey fieldstone, with four bed, three bath, living, dining and family rooms, each with fireplace, access from family room to patio and outdoor pool, with spectacular view of river valley and city." On the front lawn the agent's sign had the words I'M SOLD plastered over the top. Mercedes stood beside it, waving. Barbara waved frantically back.

"Take it easy. You'll have my eye out. And watch for that package. It's your great-aunt Lucy's Spode jug."

"You don't even care that I'll never see any of my friends again. All my past, a whole twelve years, gone. Finished. And all you care about is Aunt Lucy's rotten jug."

Her mother sighed. "I do sympathize, Barb, honestly.

3

But if you could just manage to be a little less dramatic and a bit more thoughtful, life'll be easier for both of us. It's not as if we were moving to the moon."

"It might as well be," Barbara muttered as Mom drove north, away from Willow Heights. She stared gloomily through the car window, watching the large houses become neat bungalows and blocks of imitation-Spanish apartments. Oh, Dad, how could you let Mom *do* this, she thought miserably.

"I'm getting a job in Toronto, chick."

"*Toronto*. But . . . does that mean we've got to move?"

"No. Your mother's not coming. I'm going alone."

"When'll you be back, Dad? I'm going to miss you like crazy."

"I'll write," he'd promised, dodging her question. But he hadn't written, not once. And he'd packed his bags and left in the time between her going out for a swim and lunch with Mercedes and coming home again to a house empty except for Mom.

"How could you let him go without saying goodbye to me?" she'd stormed, as if it were Mom's fault. Mom had said nothing, but her face had closed like a door slamming. Nothing had been the same since.

They'd been driving north for practically ever. Weren't they there yet? Mom stopped at the lights of a major highway and Barbara looked around. On her right was a park, with neat paths and shrubs and signs that said NO DOGS and BICYCLES PROHIBITED. On her left was a mass of factories and warehouses that must have been built fifty years or more before, when they were outside the city limits. Now the city had spread around it and it looked out of place, a sooty smudge surrounded by stucco suburbs. A

newly painted billboard proclaimed WELCOME TO WEST-
WOOD LIGHT INDUSTRIAL PARK.

Funny they should call it a park too, thought Barbara.
There isn't a tree or a blade of grass in it.

Just north of the *real* park was a new subdivision of
townhouses, identical fourplexes laid out in rows, each
with a minute square of grass in front and a clothesline
and a parking spot at the rear. Mom stopped the car in
front of one of these.

It can't be, thought Barbara. Not possibly. But it was.
The moving van was parked just ahead of them and the
men were waiting, leaning against its side having a
smoke.

Barbara struggled out from among the packages and
looked in horror at their new home. In the same space that
their house in Willow Heights had taken was a two-storey
set of four townhouses, each with a blue front door and a
picture window. The lower part was finished in stucco
and the upper in siding painted a very bright blue to
match the front door. She saw with loathing that every
fourplex was identical, except for the colour of the paint,
which, on the fourplexes nearby, was green, brown and
yellow.

When the furniture movers had gone, Barbara went
upstairs to her bedroom. The window faced west, with a
splendid view of factories and warehouses, built various-
ly of brick and stone, aluminum siding and rusty iron.
Directly across the road was a two-storey brick factory of
dirty yellow brick with a modern fluorescent sign: SMITH'S
TOOL AND DIE WORKS.

I just don't believe it. Yucky, totally, completely yucky!
She unlocked her case, unzipped her overnight bag and
emptied them both onto the bed. Dad's picture came out

on top of the pile. She picked it up to put it in the position of honour at the centre of her dressing table.

His smooth dark hair and the grey eyes were like hers, but there the resemblance ended. Dad was so wonderfully good-looking, while she was just a flat-chested twelve-year-old with braces and a dreary future.

"I do love you, Dad. I'll always love you. But why did you let this happen to me? It's all so gruesome."

She sighed heavily. That was the only word to describe the last two months — *gruesome*. Silence and stony faces. Dad slamming doors and driving off and not coming home for dinner. Mom talking to her.

"He's not coming back, Barb, didn't he *tell* you? He promised he would. Didn't you understand?"

She'd stared blankly back. "You mean . . . not ever?"

Mom had nodded, and her eyes had filled with tears, which was absolutely awful, because Mom *never* cried. Part of Barbara wanted to put her arms around her and tell her it was okay, they'd manage. But this other ugly Barbara, hurt, and embarrassed by Mom's tears, began screaming. "It's your fault. It's all your fault. How could you be so mean to Dad? How could you let him go?"

If only she could have taken her cruel words back. But there was no way. They remained, piled up like a berm to cut off traffic noise from the neighbourhood. They cut off Mom from her and her from Mom.

It was at school that she learned the truth.

"Why would your mother sell the house? My mom says she must be crazy to let it go. There's something called dower rights," said Suzanne vaguely.

"*My* Mom says Mrs. Coutts could nail him for everything he's got for what he did."

"But he didn't *do* anything. What did he do?"

Suzanne sighed. "The trouble with you, Barbara, is that you're dumb. Everyone knows your father's gone to Toronto with Kristina Marriner."

Everyone but me. It was like being stripped in public. All those inquisitive eyes and voices. Only Mercedes hadn't joined in.

"Who *is* this Kristina person?" Barb asked when they were alone after school.

"Don't you remember? The Marriners' niece. She came out in the New Year to stay with them."

"The one with the long blonde hair and the gorgeous clothes? But Mercedes, she's the same age as Charles, isn't she?"

Charles was Mercedes' elder brother, and Barbara remembered that he'd been really keen on the gorgeous niece from Toronto.

If I'd only known what was happening, if I'd paid attention, maybe I could have made Dad see that Mom and I were more important than any old Kristina Marriner. Maybe . . . But it was like a river bursting its banks. Once it began, she could do nothing to stop it. The house was sold and Mom went hunting for a cheap apartment. And even though she now knew the truth it was somehow impossible to apologize to Mom for the awful things she'd said.

Now her life was over. Dad was gone for good, she would never see Mercedes again, the house was sold, and the boredom of summer holidays alone stretched ahead of her, with nothing at the end of it but the terror of a new school.

"Barbara, *will* you come down here?"

How long had Mom been yelling? She put down the photograph and slouched to the head of the stairs. "Yeah, Mom?"

"I need you to go to the store and pick up some milk and bread."

"What, *now*?"

"Yes, *now*. Or we won't have anything for lunch."

"I don't care. I'm not hungry anyway."

"Don't be ridiculous. Get down here right now."

The sharpness in Mom's voice brought Barbara downstairs on the run. "All right, don't get in a tizzy."

"Here's five dollars and the door key."

"Where's the store?"

"There's a shopping centre just east of the park. You can't miss it. But come straight back. It's going to take us ages to straighten this mess."

"Okay, Mom." She hoped her tone of voice would let Mom know just how rotten she was feeling.

She slouched out of the house and trudged along the sidewalk, dodging the runny-nosed kids who tried to push their tricycles into her shins. There didn't seem to be a soul of her age around. Just rotten kids and a small fat boy, with glasses like bottle bottoms and an armful of books, who nearly ran into her in front of the library.

On her way back from the store she saw a guy her own age, darkish, good-looking, over in the park. She crossed the road and walked casually by, but he never even noticed her, though she was wearing her crimson short shorts and a well-fitting T-shirt. He was staring at a bunch of seagulls with the dopiest expression on his face.

Well, that does it, she thought and crossed the road again. As she fumbled with the key in the unfamiliar lock a woman appeared suddenly at her elbow and followed her into the living room, still a wilderness of packing cartons.

"Barbara, what took you so long. I . . . " Barbara's mom shot out of the kitchen and stopped, her face desperate.

The newcomer pushed past Barbara. "I'm your neighbour, Mrs. Whipple. I brought you a cake."

"Mrs. Whipple, how kind. I'm Joanna Coutts. My daughter Barbara. I'm sorry I can't ask you to sit down or. . . ."

"That's just fine. I'll pop in later for tea and a nice talk. So relieved to see no small children. The last tenants—three. Pounding up and down stairs. My nerves! But I mustn't keep you."

"Barbara, get the door for Mrs. Whipple."

"Well . . . yes . . . goodbye for now. I'll be back!"

The door swung shut and Barb's mom groaned. "Thanks a lot, chum. I really need neighbours like that."

"I couldn't help it, honestly. She just *barged* in. It's a yummy looking cake, though."

"She'll be the death of my working schedule. What on earth am I to do with her?"

"Simple. Just lock the door and ignore the phone."

"She'll know I'm in. She'll hear the typewriter."

"Who cares? Mom, I know you've been messing about with articles and stuff for years, but, well . . ."

"What's the problem?"

"Are we really going to *live* on your writing?"

Her mother laughed. "Don't look so scared. I think we can do it. I've got a contract for an educational series for TV and I'm working on a series of articles on city planning and another on crime in the west. That'll tide us over until I get some more offers. We won't starve, Barbara, I

9

promise. Only, no spare cash for movies and shopping sprees and things like that, not for a while."

"You mean *no allowance?*"

"Not until I've caught up with the first month's rent and moving expenses."

"Great! I can see this is going to be a *wonderful* summer." The words came out before she could stop them.

"Barb, I'm sorry. It just can't be helped. I expect if you look around you'll find plenty to do that doesn't cost anything."

"Like what?"

"The library. The museum. Or you could volunteer to help with the little ones in some of the park programs."

"Give me a break, Mom! Can't you get support money from Dad? Suzanne said . . . and there's the money from the house. Surely . . ."

Her mom shook her head. "It's all in the lawyers' hands right now. We'll have to wait and see. Sorry, kid."

Sorry, kid. That was it. The whole divorce business had been like that. Nobody ever asked *her.* Just, "Your father's not coming back. We'll have to sell the house. You'll understand when you're older. *Sorry, kid.*"

She had to spend the next week helping Mom empty cartons and put things away in drawers and closets, storing what wouldn't fit in the gloomy basement. There was no spare room. There was no place where Barbara could be alone except her bedroom, and that was unbearably hot after eight in the morning. There was no yard at the back, just a post for the clothesline and a place to park the car. She couldn't sun tan on the front lawn, as it was practically on the main street and she felt stupid out there in a bikini.

The nights were stuffy too. She watched late movies on television and slept in, waking up hot and headachy. She and Mom didn't talk much. Mom used to be a good friend, but ever since Dad had left she'd got edgy and mean. Like now.

"Barbara, will you please get some clothes on and come downstairs. The morning's half gone."

"There's nothing to get dressed for. There's nothing to *do*."

Silence. She could almost see Mom standing at the foot of the stairs, her hand on the banisters, counting to ten.

"There's plenty to do, like tidying your room, for instance. But right now I need you to get fifty dollars out of the green machine for me. And then you can bike on to the courier office with a manuscript. So will you please get down here."

Barbara hauled herself out of bed. She felt sticky and cross and her hair was a tangled mess. She leaned over the banister. "Oh, Mom, do I have to? What a drag. Why don't you phone the courier to pick it up?"

"Because I don't have the cash to pay him, that's why. And it's not far from the bank to the courier office."

Her patient voice got on Barbara's nerves. A good screaming match might clear the air. Sometimes she tried to provoke it, but Mom's patience hadn't broken yet.

"Can't you take it over later?"

"I *could*. But there's a deadline and I have another article to finish. Would you like to eat next month?"

"Sure . . . of course."

"Then smarten up, Barbara Coutts, or you may find out

11

what it's like to be really hungry. Get some clothes on this minute and get going!"

"Okay, okay. You don't have to get tense about it." She scrambled into shorts and a shirt, grabbed her bike, which she kept chained to a downspout at the back of the unit, and crossed 142nd Street to the bank. She got the fifty dollars from the machine, tucked Mom's card and the money safely into the pocket of her shirt and mounted her bike again.

It was the first time she had ventured into Westwood Light Industrial Park, though it was all she could see from her bedroom window. Beyond it was the wide western sky and the glory of summer sunsets, but she was never in the mood to notice them. She only saw Smith's Tool and Die Works and all that it stood for.

It was as grungy as she expected. Her bicycle tires skidded on the grit left over from last winter's sanding. Shreds of packing material scuffed beneath her wheels. She passed a waterbed warehouse, the Caterpillar depot and the old Bay warehouse. Eight long boring blocks farther on she came to the courier's office. She locked her bike, handed over the big fat envelope at the desk, signed a form and came out to find the front tire of her bike as flat as a pancake.

Rage flared and she looked around savagely for the brat who'd done it. She'd kill him, she'd take him apart. . . . But there was no one in sight. There were no sidewalks to play on, there wasn't a tree or a patch of grass. The only green things were the patches of groundsel that pushed up between the frost cracks in the pavement. This was no neighbourhood for kids.

She spun the wheel and saw the nail. Short, flat-topped, very effective.

It would be a long hot ten blocks home. It was getting on for lunch time and she hadn't even had breakfast. With a groan she wheeled the wretched bike along the side of the road, past garbage containers, oil drums, broken castings, bales of packing paper. The sun beat hotly down and the sweat ran into her eyes.

She had gone about five blocks, and the park's greenery was like an oasis another five blocks ahead, when she saw the jackrabbit. It was hopping down the centre of 113th Avenue, right through the middle of Westwood Industrial Park, as if it knew exactly where it was going. It didn't have a waistcoat and watchchain like the rabbit in *Alice in Wonderland*, but it changed Barbara's life just as drastically as if she had followed it down a hole into that magical world.

TWO

Barbara stopped and stared. At that instant a flatbed truck, laden with lumber, swung out of a yard to her left. The rabbit bolted sideways and vanished.

The Barbara who lived in Willow Heights, with dozens of friends, with piano and singing lessons on Tuesdays and Thursdays and gym every Saturday morning, wouldn't have noticed or cared a hoot about the rabbit's disappearance. But the new Barbara, bored and lonely, crossed the street to see where the rabbit had got to.

The south side of 113th Avenue consisted of flat-faced warehouses, built terrace-fashion right along the block, with no cross streets between 142nd Street and 149th Street. There was nowhere for the rabbit to go, except in through an open door. And there were no open doors.

The toe of her sandal caught in something and she clutched her bike for support. Down among the grit and groundsel was a gleam of metal. A steel rail. The remains

14

of an early railway line, covered by the tarmac paving of 113th Avenue, but reappearing as the ghost of a spur line that vanished into a narrow passage that tunneled between the terraced warehouses. She was in time to see the rabbit hop briskly into a patch of sunshine at the far end of the passage.

She looked up. The warehouses on either side of the spur line were joined together at the second storey. HODGSON AND was stenciled in faded yellow on the dirty red brick of the warehouse to her left. CAMPBELL was stenciled above the arch, while AND SONS LTD completed the name on the building to her right.

It wasn't a marble archway — the walls of the passage were grimy brick — but beyond the shadows something glittered silvery and magically enticing. Barbara propped her bike against the wall and plunged into the darkness.

Dirt had settled between the ties, and pigweed and groundsel grew in wiry tufts. She stepped from tie to tie. With each step the noise of trucks, chain saws and jack hammers faded. Then, tantalizingly, there was a fence across the passage, blocking her way. It was more than two metres high, too tall to see over, but one of the wooden slats was loose at the bottom. The gap was too narrow for her to squeeze through, though big enough for a jackrabbit. She crouched down on the weedy ground and pushed her face close to the gap.

A bewilderment of blue and yellow, white and green, met her eye. The heady smell of sunwarmed honey. It's a secret garden, she thought. No, that's impossible. Probably the yard of a warehouse in the next block, full of rusty machinery and old tires.

Her mind hovered between forgetting it and going

home for lunch, or staying to explore. The idea of pushing that dumb bike home was so unattractive that exploring became more enticing by the second. She tried to push another slat loose, but the fence had been solidly made with the nails toed in so that their bent tops bit into the wood. Only a split had caused one slat to loosen.

The cross bars were on the far side, of course, so there was nothing to get a foothold on this side. She reached up, but couldn't touch the top. The wall of the right-hand warehouse, the AND SONS LTD one, was trimmed with a double layer of bricks in a kind of step design. The bricks stood out almost a centimetre. A toehold!

Just a look, to see if it's a real garden or a weedy lot.

Barbara spat on her hands and rubbed them against her white shorts. Her right toe *here*, her left foot to push up against the fence and a two-handed grab at the top. She breathed in, thought it through just like she would in gym class, and leapt. Her right toe found the brick ledge. Her left boosted her up and her hands caught the flat top of the fence. She heaved and got a leg over. And stared.

She was looking into the boughs of a young aspen. Its leaves, twisting in the slight breeze, had shone silvery even through the shadows of the passage. The patch of ground beyond was surrounded on all four sides by warehouses, blind surfaces of dirty red or yellow. Their walls enclosed an oblong, perhaps twelve by ten metres, of untouched bush. It blazed with branching clover, white and yellow, and with blue, white and purple flowers and a patch of orange poppies.

Barbara swung herself over the fence and climbed down on the far side, finding easy footholds on the cross bars of the fence. She turned and found herself staring into the terrified eyes of the jackrabbit. It had backed into the farthest corner and was standing, frozen, on its hind legs, its brown ear tips erect above the tall grass, a branch of clover still in its mouth.

Slowly she slid to the ground and sat with her back against the gap in the fence. From this viewpoint the wild flowers were at eye level. The smell of hot nectar was dizzying. Bumblebees blundered noisily from branch to branch of the high clover. A dragonfly, as enormous as a pterodactyl from this new perspective, darted to and fro across the garden. Quiet slowly seeped in and her heart-beats slowed. The rabbit's ears relaxed. It dropped back onto all fours and went on munching.

A real secret garden, she thought. Mine and the rabbit's. Perhaps I could tame him, so he wouldn't be frightened of me, so I'd have company.

She looked slowly around. As well as the aspen, there were two fair-sized maples against the western ware-house wall. The grass was calf-high. If she could find something to hold water she could build a pool in the middle, a pool to reflect the sky and bring even more light into the garden. Then the birds would come. She could build a bird table to tempt the sparrows and chickadees. Peanuts for the blue jays.

In the ravine behind her old house there were always birds singing and squirrels scolding from the big stand of spruce and pine, aspen and cottonwood. In the back garden there had been a big mountain ash, weighed down with clusters of berries. The waxwings loved that tree. They would arrive suddenly in flocks of two or three hundred birds to gorge on the berries and then, as a kind of rude thank-you, leave red droppings like blood spatters all over the driveway and Dad's white Lincoln Continental.

In the new townhouse complex there seemed to be no birds at all, except for the occasional sparrows squabbling in the gutter. Because there were no trees. Nothing but rows and rows of houses, each with its small square lawn and border of geranium and dusty miller.

Barbara suddenly noticed that the sun had moved right across the secret garden. She glanced at her watch, the Seiko that Dad had given her for her birthday last October. He hadn't been able to get to her party, but he'd had the watch sent over to the house by the jeweller. It was smarter than anyone else's in Grade Six.

Now she stared at it. *Two-fifteen?* It couldn't be! It should only have taken her half an hour at most to get to the courier office and back. Would Mom believe that the flat tire had delayed her that long? She could tell Mom about the secret garden, of course, but . . .

In that instant she made up her mind that the garden was hers, and hers alone.

She climbed the fence and walked as fast as she dared over the ties to where she had left her bike. No one had seen it. This wasn't a street for pedestrians. There was nothing to come for and no sidewalk to walk on. Her secret garden was safe.

Her mind full of sweet nectar and the hum of bees, she pushed the bike home, trying to think of a good excuse for being so late, if Mom should challenge her. But it was all right. When she opened the door she could hear the clatter of Mom's typewriter. She slid silently upstairs, washed her filthy hands and knees, dropped her once white shorts and T-shirt into the hamper, and came downstairs in clean clothes, with her long hair neatly brushed.

Mom's breakfast dishes were in the sink and nothing had been done for lunch. Evidently the morning had sped by for Mom as it had for her, so her luck was in. She eased open the refrigerator, got out a carton of eggs and stirred four of them in a pan. She put bread in the toaster and filled the kettle.

"Mom, you must be starving — it's nearly three o'clock."

"What? Barb, you startled me! I didn't hear you come in."

"I didn't want to disturb you," Barbara said meekly — a bit too meekly, she realized when Mom looked at her sharply. "Anyway," she went on quickly, "I've made scrambled eggs on toast. Can I move these papers over?"

"No, don't touch them. I don't want them muddled. They're my notes on an article on the Canadian penal system. And, talking of reform, you've actually made lunch! How very nice. Would I be looking at a reformed daughter?"

"Something like that, I guess."

"You actually *look* different. Kind of sparkly. You're not up to anything awful, are you?"

"Goodness, no. Why should I be?"

"I don't know. Forgive my suspicious nature. The transformation is a bit startling, that's all. But I'm delighted. Maybe when I've finished work today we could have a treat — bike down to the river for a picnic supper, maybe?"

"I've got a nail in my tire."

"Then fix it, helpless! That was a great lunch, thanks.

I'll keep my coffee and get back to work."

She sat brooding over her typewriter, her coffee mug in her hands, leaving Barbara to remove the dishes, do the washing up and spend a frustrating afternoon out back prying the bicycle tire off its rim, patching the inner tube, testing it in the kitchen sink and putting the whole thing back together again.

In the process she collected a crowd of very small children who got their fingers caught in the spokes and fought over who should get to hold the tire iron. She hadn't seen one single kid older than six in the whole of Westwood Acres. Nobody her own age.

"There'll be school," Mom had said when Barb complained of being lonely, but she didn't want to think about school. Grade Seven. Junior High. She'd be a total loner and everyone else would already be friends for years. Nobody left but the wimps and the brains, and she didn't want to be part of either group, thanks. Life was really rotten.

She rescued the tire iron from the smallest kid before he bopped someone on the head with it. He bellowed loudly and a mother appeared at her kitchen door and stared accusingly at Barbara. She wheeled the bike around to the front and poked her head in at the door. Mom was still typing.

"I'll just go for a spin to make sure it's okay."

Mom waved vaguely. "I'll be through in half an hour. Better give me my bank card and change and the courier's receipt before we forget."

Barbara's hand went automatically to her shirt pocket — panic! She thundered upstairs and pulled all the clothes out of the laundry hamper. Suppose she'd dropped the money or the card in the garden? But they were all right, safely folded into the breast pocket of the T-shirt she'd worn that morning. She bundled the clothes back into the hamper and ran downstairs.

She suddenly realized how desperately important it was that the garden should remain secret. She thought about it as she rode around the block. It would probably be safer to walk there, because if someone *were* to see her bike, even parked in the dark alley, it would give her away completely. As bad as footprints in the snow.

She promised herself that she would go to the garden on foot from now on, and be extra careful that no one saw her duck down the passage. But now she had to put it out of her mind and concentrate on the picnic. She spent the evening trying to be cheerful and entertaining.

I certainly fooled Mom, she thought when they got home after a barbecue supper of sausages in the park. Maybe I'm destined to be a great actress some day. But Mom put a hand on her forehead and said, "I do hope you're not sickening for something. You've been acting oddly all day. Is anything on your mind?"

"Not a thing, Mom."

"Not *really* worried about school, are you?"

THREE

September the second arrived faster than Barbara had believed possible.

"I won't know a single person," she wailed. "They'll all despise me. And I don't know what to wear." She tore off her shirt and designer jeans and threw them on the floor.

"Hurry up, Barb, you're going to be late. Surely it's not that important what you wear?"

Important? she thought gloomily, it's *crucial*. Suppose they're all wearing jeans and I turn up in a dress? Or the other way round. I'll be *branded*. In Willow Heights I used to phone Mercedes the night before and we'd plan exactly what to wear. I wish I were back.

"You just don't understand," she said aloud.

"I do really. Now put those jeans back on, they're fine, and come down for breakfast."

"I couldn't eat a thing. I'd just throw up." Barbara

22

followed her mother gloomily downstairs. "I'll have a cup of coffee."

"But you hate coffee."

"I know, but it feels like the right thing for the first day of Junior High. Kind of symbolic, like a rite of passage. . . . Yuck, how can you drink this stuff?"

"I guess it grows on one. Now, have you got everything?"

"I think so. Don't fuss, Mom, you're making me nervous. Well, goodbye. Wish me luck."

"Break a leg!"

Barbara couldn't help a reluctant smile as she walked down the road, remembering the expression on Mercedes' face the first time she'd heard Mom say that. She had to explain that Mom had been involved in a theatre group, where saying "good luck" to someone was the most unlucky thing you could do.

The smile carried her to within a block of the new school. Then it vanished and terror took its place. She slowed down to a crawl, planning to reach the door just as the bell rang.

She followed the crowd in and found herself at last in the third row of the Grade Seven classroom, with a view of a boring suburban street on her left and, on her right, of the dopey-looking boy she had seen staring at the seagulls in the park. Just my luck, she thought gloomily. His name, she learned from the attendance roll, was Stan Natyshyn. Beyond him was the small fat boy she'd bumped into outside the library, called Terry something. Pretty scary. But in front were a couple of nice-looking girls in jeans. Thank goodness I wore jeans, Barb thought. One of the girls was called Alison and the other. . . .

Her own name was called and she had to stand up, with

twenty-eight strange pairs of eyes staring at her, and be introduced as the new girl. She could feel herself turn red, and all the eyes seemed hostile or uncaring. As soon as she could she slumped down in her desk and put up a barrier of indifference around her and silently dared her new classmates to break it down. Nobody bothered. The day passed with agonizing slowness.

"How did it go?" her mother asked when she tramped into the house at the end of the afternoon.

"Quietly."

"That's a novel description of the first day of school."

"Nobody said a single word to me all day. No, I'm wrong. A boy called Terry apologized when he bumped into me in the door."

"It'll get better, honey. You know it will. But you'll have to meet them halfway."

"Why should I?" Barbara snapped and stamped upstairs to her own room.

"Do hush, Barb! You're heavier on your feet than an elephant. Please try. Mrs. Whipple's been complaining again. She says you're as noisy as all the previous children combined."

"I apologize for living."

"And don't overreact. There's only a thin wall between the units. Poor Mrs. Whipple has her rights too."

"Yeah, I know." She hung over the banister, suddenly needing to ask. "Mom, is Dad still in Toronto?"

"As far as I know."

"I thought he'd write. Just to wish me luck on the first day of school, you know?"

She knew she should stop, that she was just hurting Mom, but it had been a rotten day, and maybe she wanted

24

Mom to share the rottenness of it.

"Why hasn't he written?" she persisted. "He prom-ised."

"He didn't pay much attention to how you were doing in school even when we lived in the same house. I don't know why you'd expect him to change now."

Mom's words were like icicles that hung coldly in the air between them. Barbara crept upstairs and dumped her books on the bed. She was tempted to fling herself down on the bed too and have a good orgy of crying, but she found she felt angry rather than sad. Angry at Mom and Dad for breaking up a comfortable family, for forcing her to leave Willow Heights and go to a creepy new school in a creepy neighbourhood. They don't care about me, she thought. No one does.

On impulse she grabbed her purse and ran to the bus depot. With two changes of bus, it took over an hour to get down to Willow Heights. She walked slowly along the familiar street. Someone else was already living in their house. There was a baby buggy under the shade tree in front and a strange car parked in the driveway. She turned her head and walked quickly past, then ran up the steps next door and rang the bell.

"Barbara! What a surprise. I was expecting . . ."

"Hi, Mercedes. I thought I'd just drop by. In the neighbourhood, you know. How've you been?"

"Great. Er, come on in. I thought you were Suzanne. She'll be over in a minute, I guess."

"It's terrific seeing you again. Did you have a good holiday?"

"It was fabulous, thanks. Suzanne's bringing over her photos, so we can compare."

"When did you get back? You said you'd phone."

Barb saw Mercedes blush. "I guess about a week ago. But Mom and I have been busy getting new clothes and school supplies and stuff. You know what it's like."

"Sure."

Then Suzanne arrived. "Hi, Barbara. Fancy seeing you back here! How are you enjoying life on the north side?"

"Just fine, thanks." Barbara was uncomfortably aware of Suzanne's eyes on her hair, cut by Mom in the kitchen instead of at an expensive hair salon, and on her last year's jeans, just a bit too short.

They sat in the family room and, after Mercedes brought cookies and soft drinks, they looked at the holiday photographs of Greece and the Caribbean and of a cottage in Maine twice the size of Barbara's townhouse in Westwood. Suzanne and Mercedes vied with each other as to who had had the greatest time.

". . . and what about *you*, Barbara?" Mercedes remembered her at last. "What's your new school like?"

Barbara looked up from the photographs of Greek temples and the cruise ship and managed a bright smile. "Just great. I know two guys already. Stan and Terry. And a neat girl called Alison."

"I just don't know how you've survived, honestly, Barbara. You didn't get to go away *all* summer, did you? What a shame. You must have been bored out of your mind."

Bored? For an instant she felt like pouring out the misery of Westwood Acres and the horror of her new school. But as she looked at her old friends, sitting cosily side by side on the sofa, shutting her out, she knew that all she'd get from them would be pity, and she couldn't stand that.

"Actually I had a terrific summer. I found—" She

stopped. Showing off had become such a habit in Willow Heights that now she was back she had almost given away the secret garden. She looked at her watch and stood up. "Got to go or I'll be late for supper. Great seeing you again."

Riding home on the bus, changing at the terminal and riding again, Barbara thought miserably about Mercedes. They'd been best friends since kindergarten, but Mercedes hadn't even phoned, though she'd been home for a week. And she *had* promised.

I suppose I could have called her again, she thought. But when I tried, the phone just rang and rang. It's not just *that*, not phoning. They were ashamed of me, like I didn't belong there any more. Well, tough. I don't care. And I don't care if I never see Mercedes again either. She blotted her eyes surreptitiously with her fingers, hoping no one on the bus would notice.

It might have been all right if she hadn't had to wait so long for the second bus, but she was hardly in the house before Mom was on her case.

"Where *have* you been? I've been worried sick."

"I just went over to see Mercedes, that's all. The buses took forever." She looked critically around the tiny living-dining room, not noticing her mother's expression soften.

"I'd have driven you over if I'd known you wanted — "

"You wouldn't have had time. You never have time any more. Look at this place, Mom, it's the total pits. Couldn't you do something to make it nicer if we've *got* to live here?"

In the silence that followed she looked up. "What's the matter? What did I say now?"

Mom sighed. "Forget it. Wash your hands and come to supper. But I warn you, macaroni cheese doesn't improve with being kept warm for an hour."

Nag, nag, thought Barbara miserably, as she wrestled with the stodgy casserole. After she'd helped with the dishes, in a silence cold enough to make ice cubes, she stomped upstairs and looked gloomily out the window, at Smith's Tool and Die Works. How ugly it all looked. Yet within it, like a kind of magic, lay the secret garden. Campbell's Bush. Yes, *that* was still hers. Hers and nobody else's. So nobody could spoil it or take it from her, as her other life had been taken. She slid downstairs past the rattle of the typewriter and out of the house. She ran across the road and along 113th Avenue, running from school and Mom's lack of understanding and, more than the rest, from the silence where Dad should be.

Campbell's Bush was magic. In the shadow of the passage, walking the ties towards the light at the end, she could feel herself getting lighter too. By the time she had climbed the fence she had shed the disagreeable Barbara as a snake sheds its skin.

She walked slowly around her domain, remembering and discovering. The maples were beginning to turn and the aspen's leaves were like old gold. The poppies had been bitten by a touch of early frost, and the bees had left.

She explored the garden thoroughly, surprised to find out that the spur line didn't finish at the fence, but crossed the garden, invisible beneath the grass and flowers. It turned left at the southern end of the garden and ended beneath the blank wall of the factory to the east.

How odd. She looked up at the dirty yellow bricks and, at that precise moment, the western sun etched in shadow, like a dark line, the outline of double doors above a loading bay. Once, long ago, when the city was young, this factory must have stood alone in the middle of the bush, with the railway line from the main tracks from the north feeding it with raw materials and picking up whatever was being made. Later on another warehouse must have been built flush against its western end, and still later Hodgson and Campbell and their sons had put up the brick warehouse to the north.

The railway must still have been in use then, or the track would have been ripped up and there would have been no need for the passage. But later the roads in the north of the city were paved, and trucks became more important than trains to feed the industrial park with raw materials and take away the finished goods. The track fell into disuse. The space between the buildings was forgotten. The fence had been put up to stop tramps, and now even that was history. Seeds blew and seedlings grew and the rain and snow nurtured the forgotten bush and turned it into a secret garden.

Forgotten. That was the key word. It could be maybe fifty years since the bush was enclosed. Forgotten. Secret. Until she, Barbara Coutts, had discovered it. Except . . .

She stood beneath the concrete slab of the loading bay and looked up at the double doors, biting her lip. The paint was blistered, coming off in tatters and flakes, like sunburned skin. It hadn't been touched in years and years. But that didn't prove anything.

Suppose the people on the other side of the wall knew all about the secret place? Suppose on hot days they threw open the double doors and let the honey-sweet air of *her* garden into the stuffy office or factory within?

["\n\n\n\n\n\n\n\n\n\n\n\n\n\n\n\n\n\n\n\n\n\n\n\n"]

["\n\n\n\n\n\n\n\n\n\n\n\n\n\n\n\n\n\n\n\n\n\n\n\n"]

She felt as Columbus might have felt if he'd landed on Trinidad and been met by a representative from the Holiday Inn. If those doors were ever opened, if they might be opened, then there was no magic and she had discovered nothing.

She couldn't bear to stay any longer. She scrambled over the fence and ran as quickly as she dared along the ties. It was chilly out of the sun, in the shadow of the passage, and she wrapped her arms across her chest and shivered. I *have* to find out what's behind those doors. Only how?

FOUR

By Saturday Barbara had worked out a strategy. She surprised her mother by coming down early for breakfast. Then she remembered that the stores on 111th Avenue wouldn't be open for another hour, so she surprised her mother even more by doing the breakfast dishes and tidying her room.

"Are you sure you're all right, dear?"

"Just great, Mom. I'm off now, okay?"

She walked fast down the western edge of the park towards 111th Avenue. This was one of the main arteries of the city, leading to the mountains and the west coast. Its southern side held back wildly multiplying rows of stucco and frame houses, each with its crabapple or mayday tree, its rows of tomatoes and corn. The northern side of the highway was the southern limit of Westwood Industrial Park. It was lined with offices, factories and warehouses, and somewhere along its dusty shabbiness was a yellow

31

brick factory or warehouse with an ell-shaped plan and a loading bay that opened onto the secret garden.

Barbara had counted exactly how many steps it took to walk from the passage to 142nd Street. If she walked exactly as far along 111th Avenue, she should finish up in front of the building that backed onto the secret garden. But like so many excellent plans, it didn't quite work out. A city crew was digging up the road around a fire hydrant. There were hoses and piles of subsoil clay. There were back hoes. By the time she had dodged around the disaster she had lost count of her steps.

There were now three possibilities. The first was a carpet remnant store with the words CASH AND – ARRY on a cotton banner above the entrance. She tried to imagine the men who owned the store. They would be Cash (as in Johnny) and his brother Harry. Or maybe his name was Barry. Or Larry. No, not Larry. Larry was Dad's name, and she didn't want to think about him or this lovely day would be ruined.

She wandered into the store as if she were looking for someone and went quickly out again before Cash (or Barry) could try to sell her some carpet. She had seen at a glance that the store's back wall was as straight as a ruler from east to west. There was no secret garden hidden behind it.

The next store but one was a lumber yard with a warehouse behind it. It turned out to be great fun, with piles of two-by-fours and sheets of plywood, all smelling of spruce and pine in the already hot sun. Inside the warehouse were rows of bins containing every kind of nail, screw, clip and bracket you could ever possibly want. She wandered unnoticed around the bins, since the store was packed with weekend craftsmen in caps that said

"O'Keefe" or "Blue Jays," all of them poking into the bins and inspecting the racks of lumber, working her way to the back wall. It was completely flat with a loading bay on the left, a big truck pulled up in front of it.

The store in the middle she had left to the end, because it was a very different proposition. In the past few years some quite expensive furniture stores had abandoned downtown, where the rents were too high, and moved into renovated warehouses in areas like Westwood Industrial Park.

Teak For All was one of these. Its windows gleamed in the morning sun and its door pull was of polished brass. Inside Barbara glimpsed a wonderful desk with a pulldown front and dozens of little drawers and cubicles, just like the one Mom had once said she'd give her eye-teeth to own.

"What on earth do you need a great desk like that for?" Dad had said. "After all, you don't have to *do* anything. My accountant looks after all the bills."

"For my writing," Mom had said softly, and Barbara had wanted to beg Dad to give her the desk. But she'd said nothing. He'd been awfully bad-tempered if ever she entered the grown-up conversations, so she'd bitten her lip and listened to him say, "I'm not made of money, thank you very much," and Mom had snapped back, "Well, I don't know what you spend it on then, your secretaries, maybe?" Then she'd looked at Barbara and whispered, "Sorry, sorry." Mom and Dad hadn't talked for a week after that.

Don't think about them, she told herself. Concentrate. She peered through the window. There was a sofa upholstered in white leather. Expensive coffee tables like the ones in their old house. The back of the store was lost in shadow, and between it and the front hovered the salesmen — she counted four — all with three-piece suits and very smooth hair.

She jittered to and fro outside the door, feeling irritatingly young. It was maddening to be twelve, neither one thing nor the other. At twelve you were expected to be totally responsible, like helping in the house and always phoning when you were going to be late home; but if you used eyeshadow or bought crazy earrings or yearned for a black party dress with a slit up the back everyone said: You're too young.

She looked doubtfully down at her blue jeans and the T-shirt that said I'M ADDICTED TO WEST EDMONTON MALL. If she were only wearing a black dress and those parrot earrings she wouldn't think twice before walking into a store like this.

"Would you excuse us, please."

Barbara jumped and turned. A couple was waiting patiently for her to move out of the way.

"Sorry." She stood aside and politely held open the door for them. They were about the age of Mom and Dad. About the age of . . . Impulsively she followed them in, trying to look meek and bored, like a daughter on a shopping expedition.

A salesman instantly stepped forward. "May I be of assistance?"

They moved away, talking. Barbara admired the woman's suit of rough creamy material, with a pale silk blouse and an amber necklace. Instantly she abandoned her dream of a black dress and parrot earrings and saw herself in cream and silk and amber.

Making herself as invisible as possible, she followed

the couple and their salesman. Barbara was quite good at being invisible. It was done by keeping her elbows close to her body and by breathing slowly and not too deeply. She kept her eyes down — it was important not to catch other people's eyes when you were invisible — and shot quick secret glances to right and left as the others, with her tailing invisibly behind, threaded their way through the displays of furniture.

The couple took ages to pick out what they liked, but Barb didn't dare move far away from them and explore. She noticed that as soon as she got a certain distance from them a kind of radar caused one of the other salesmen to move towards her, like a bloodhound on the trail, invisible though she was.

At last the couple made up their minds and were ushered to the back of the store. Finally Barbara was going to find out just how secret her secret garden was. Her heart beat fast and she walked eagerly after them. The salesman half turned and she slowed down and lapsed into invisibility again.

At the northeast corner of the store there was indeed a very deep ell, stacked with crated furniture. To the right was a double door that must open onto a laneway beside the building. She looked anxiously to the left. Here a small office had been built within the ell. On its back wall, the one facing west, was a large framed poster of the mermaid in Copenhagen Harbour.

Barbara grinned and cast off her cloak of invisibility. It was all right! The garden was hers and nobody else's. In fact it would add an extra spice to know that behind the double doors of the abandoned loading bay was a sales office with a poster of Copenhagen Harbour and that behind it everyone was working like mad to make money, not knowing that on the other side of the wall flowers were growing like crazy.

As she ran out of the store, she heard the salesman say, "Now may I show you something for your daughter's room? We have a delightful line in—"

"Daughter? We don't have a daughter."

Barbara skipped along the edge of the highway, dodging the back hoe, the hoses and the muddy ditch. She was Columbus casting anchor in the West Indies, Cortez wildly surmising on his peak in Darien, Neil Armstrong ... "One giant step for mankind," she muttered as she leapt the ditch. The garden was hers and hers alone and she was going to make it perfect.

After the first few horrible days, school was shaping up pretty well. Thursday and Monday were Phys Ed days. The gym was at least as good as the one at Willow Heights, which was a surprise, and Mrs. Rawlings, the teacher, had once actually won a bronze in the Commonwealth Games.

It was fun to do something really well. Barbara forgot about being self-conscious and despising the new school. It was gratifying to feel the stir among the watching students when she did a perfect routine on the bars and stood, arms spread, before making a professional landing.

A few of the others weren't bad, but Stan Natyshyn was truly embarrassing. He fell off the beam every time he tried to stand upright, and he tripped on his approach to the vaulting horse so that he landed across it with a smack that must have hurt like heck.

He laughed it off, but Barbara couldn't help feeling a bit

sorry for him. It must be tough to be such a klutz. A pity, too, because he wasn't bad looking, tall and slim, with soulful dark eyes and dark hair swept back like in *Dr. Zhivago*.

But he *was* a klutz, and he stammered when he got upset. Then the kids giggled at him. She decided she'd better steer clear of him. Nothing was worse for one's social life than being stuck with the class dolt.

When the recess bell rang and they began to clear away the equipment, Mrs. Rawlings asked Barbara to stay behind.

"I'm coaching a small group for the provincial games. Would you like to try out?"

"*Provincial*, wow! Actually I *was* taking gym at the gym club."

"Are you going on with that?"

"No."

"Hmm. Were you any good?"

"Not bad, I guess." She laughed, trying to keep her voice upbeat.

"So why did you quit?"

Barbara hesitated. She could feel her face getting red.

"I'm not interested in quitters," Mrs. Rawlings went on.

"I didn't. There's no money for extras any more, that's all."

"Bad luck. Well, Barbara, what about putting your energy into school gym? We don't have all the facilities of the gym club, but it's not bad here at Westwood. We use the twenty minutes of recess after regular class on Phys Ed days, since we're already warmed up, and we have an extra hour after school on Wednesdays. Could you handle that?"

"I'd love it. Thank you." She felt herself flushing and stared down at the floor. "Will it cost much? I don't know . . ."

"You'll need a practice costume for now, that's all."

"I've got a maillot and tights."

"Without feet?"

"Yes."

"Then that's all right. Stay behind with the others on Monday. I think you'll enjoy the challenge, even if you don't make the trials in October."

Suddenly Barbara found that she had broken through the invisible wall separating the old and new kids. After the Wednesday workout they all went over to the Dairy Queen for a shake and she got to know Alison and Jessica, who were also in Grade Seven, as well as the others on the team.

She skipped home, humming joyfully, full of milk-shake. "Mom are you there?" The dining ell was empty and the typewriter covered. She ran upstairs and bumped into Mom coming out of the bathroom. Her eyes were red and swollen.

"Mom?"

"I've got a bit of a headache. I'll lie down with an Aspirin for half an hour."

"I'll make dinner."

"There's leftover beef. We just need a salad."

"I — " Barbara swallowed the words "I hate leftover beef" and said "I'll wash the lettuce" instead.

At supper she noticed that her mom was working hard at being cheerful and was far more chatty than normal.

"What's up?"

"Nothing. Why?"

"I'm a big girl now, Mom. You can tell me. Are we broke? Or is it Dad? There's nothing wrong with Dad, is there?"

"No, nothing like that. It's just that I had a session with my lawyer today and the long and short of it is that your father says he won't contest the divorce in any way or fight my having full custody, so long as I make no claims on the property."

"But it was his fault, wasn't it? Mercedes said . . . Mom, does that mean he'd rather have the money than me?"

"I don't think he'd see it like that, honey. It's me he wants to hurt, not you."

"But *why?*"

"It's pretty complicated, Barb, but I think he would rather hate me than feel guilty."

Barbara was going to say that was dumb when she remembered having the same kind of feelings, being mean to Mom because she felt rotten herself. "Are we going to manage?"

"We'll get by. He's bound to pay maintenance, though that's hard to enforce with him living in a different province. My lawyer thinks I'm crazy to let it go without a fight, but I know Larry better than he does. I just don't want you getting caught in the middle, getting hurt. I know you're better off living with me, even if you are short of spending money. I'm determined that if he leaves us alone we won't ask him for anything, except your basic maintenance. I've got enough work to see us through the next couple of months. And so it goes." Her voice wobbled. "I hope I made the right choice, kid."

"It's okay, Mom." This time Barbara was able to hug her. "We'll manage. We've got each other."

Mom tried to laugh. "I'll remind you of that the next

time you ask for designer jeans and I have to say no."

It wasn't until she was in bed that night that what Mom had really been saying came home to her. She wasn't going to be staying with Dad. Not even seeing him. No, that couldn't be right. It was only Mom he didn't want to see and vice versa. He'd come and see *her*. He was bound to. There was her thirteenth birthday in October, and there was Christmas . . .

She told Alison and Jessica about it, in strictest confidence, and found to her surprise that Jessica's parents were also divorced, and that Alison made up for happily married parents by having a cousin who had been part of a custody battle.

". . . and one time Uncle Jim kidnapped Marianne and got her as far as Montreal before the police caught him."

"Wow! What happened?"

"Uncle Jim was put in jail overnight and Marianne got a free flight back to Vancouver. But she never got the chance to see Montreal."

Kidnapping! No wonder Mom wanted to cut away cleanly with no fuss or muss. Though it seemed unlikely that Dad would ever kidnap *her* when he hadn't even asked for visiting privileges. She asked Alison about that.

"Well, my mother said that with Uncle Jim, it was because he was the sort of person who always wanted what he didn't have, and that's why he was such a successful businessman. But I think he must have been crazy. My cousin Marianne is the drippiest kid I've ever known."

They were interrupted by the recess bell and went in to art class. Barbara looked forward to it, as she'd always done well at the Willow Heights school, her work being neat and without painty fingermarks.

Mrs. Machenko disagreed. She held up Barbara's assignment. "So stiff!" She gestured with a hand extravagantly laden with silver and turquoise rings. "Loosen up, child. Stop drawing these terrible still lifes. Still, yes. Life, no! Give me something fresh, something that's important to you, yes?"

"I can't think of anything," Barbara muttered. Not a word about how neat her work was. Or how like a jug the jug looked. Well, the woman was nuts anyway. Look at all those rings. And paint under her fingernails.

"Of course you can. Bring me a sketch next week. All of you." She whirled around on the class in a tangle of homespun and ceramic beads. "None of you are any good. All so tight, so *prissy*. So you can stop laughing at this Barbara here. Only Stanislaus is any good. Draw for me like Stanislaus, yes?"

She held up a pencil sketch and Barbara felt a sudden jolt as if her secret inner self had somehow been laid bare. Because the sketch was of a jackrabbit—*her* rabbit. Alive from its inquisitive ears to the frail whiskers around its twitchy nose.

"Ahhh!" There was a spontaneous reaction from the class, which the boys instantly tried to turn into a joke.

"Oh, look at the dear little bunny wabbit!"

"Is that your pet bunny, Stanislaus?"

Crimson-faced, Stan snatched the sketch from the teacher's hand. "P-please, Mrs. Machenko, my name is *Stan*."

"Stan? You call yourself Stan, when you have a beautiful name like Stanislaus? A hero's name! A saint's name!"

The class exploded, and even Barbara joined in the laughter. It was such a relief to be one of the crowd, laughing with the others. Only the fat Terry was silent and indignant, while Stan slumped down behind his desk, red and speechless. Afterwards she wished she hadn't laughed, because she really needed to talk to Stan.

"Hey, Stan. Where did you draw that rabbit?"

He looked at her vaguely, without answering.

"Look, I'm sorry I laughed, but I need to know. Where did you see it?"

"The r-rabbit? Over in the park. He's hard to find sometimes, but he likes the p-peony bushes by the swimming pool. There are larch trees close by and I think he scavenges for seeds."

"That's all right then." She saw his puzzled expression and went on hastily, "You draw awfully well. I could feel his fur and whiskers just as if he was real."

"That's not hard, just a trick really. The important thing is really using your eyes, not just drawing what you think a rabbit looks like."

"Huh?"

"Well, look how most people draw faces. They think they're looking at the model, but they don't really see him. Then they draw a round head with an ear on each side and two eyes near the top with a nose and mouth under it. And then they wonder why it looks like a little kid's drawing. You've got to really look. Then just relax and put down what you've seen."

Barbara noticed that when Stan talked about drawing

he didn't stammer at all and his vague eyes sparkled with enthusiasm.

"You make it sound so easy."

"It is. Just relax and look. You'll be okay."

"Thanks. Now all I have to do is think of a subject!"

The next six days went by at lightning speed, what with school, gym practice and homework. Whenever Barbara thought about her art assignment she pushed it to the back of her mind. Later. I'll do it when I've got more time, she promised herself.

"I can't think of anything that's important to me except maybe gym and there's no way I could draw a person performing," she confessed to Alison and Jessica on the way home from late gym class.

Alison giggled. "I've done mine."

"What did you draw?"

"John McMichael."

Barbara and Jessica collapsed against each other and screamed with laughter.

"He'll kill you!" Jessica gasped at last.

"So'll Mrs. Machenko, I bet. Did you make his ears stick out? They do, you know."

They parted at the corner, and Barbara ran the rest of the way home, thundered upstairs, remembered Mrs. Whipple halfway and tiptoed up the rest of the flight. Downstairs the typewriter rattled away like volley after volley of machine-gun fire. She decided she couldn't possibly study with all that racket going on, so she grabbed her binder and her French textbook and set out for Campbell's Bush.

The leaves of the aspen no longer flashed silver from

the darkness of the passageway. Those few that remained were gold and dry. Today's the twenty-first of September, she remembered. Two days to the autumnal equinox. Winter's on the way.

"The year is winding down," she said out loud, feeling grown-up and pleasantly melancholy. Maybe she should write poetry this year. If she were to die young they would find her notebooks hidden in her room, filled with deathless verse, all about how miserable Dad and Mom had made her. Or she might stay alive and become rich and famous. Was it possible to become rich by writing poetry?

She went over to the beat-up cooler, which she'd picked up at a garage sale, and hauled over to Campbell's Bush. She took out fresh birdseed for the feeder. The sparrows and chickadees had busily kicked most of the old seed onto the ground, where it lay in a mound at her feet. That'll sprout a funny crop next spring, she thought, and she wondered if she could build a rim around the feeding table to discourage such extravagance, but she came up against the usual problem of having no tools. Assembling the feeder had been enough of a job, with only Mom's all-purpose screwdriver.

With the housekeeping done, she relaxed in her favourite corner, her back against the sun-warmed concrete of the loading bay. She fished out a chocolate bar from the cooler — milk chocolate with raisins — and ate it slowly, square by square, letting the chocolate melt and saving the raisins to chew in a lovely wodge at the end.

She was half asleep when she saw the grass move. Two dark-tipped ears appeared like two strange brown leaves close to the fence. She froze, breathing as quietly as she could.

The jackrabbit hopped briskly across the garden to the pile of discarded seed and began to munch, now and then lifting his head for a cautious look around. His stomach grew visibly rounder as Barb watched. You be careful, or you won't be able to get back under the fence, she warned him silently, and smiled. The birdseed wasn't going to be wasted after all. She wouldn't fuss about a rim for the feeder.

Impulsively she turned to a clean page in her binder and began to sketch. Her first try was a total disaster. It didn't even look like a stuffed rabbit. Hey, that's neat. Stuffed rabbit, as in rabbit stuffed with seed. She turned to a fresh page. This wasn't nearly as bad. She told herself that she wasn't actually *drawing* the rabbit, but making studies for a drawing. Real artists did that and they usually looked like nothing particular, except for Leonardo da Vinci, of course, and she wasn't even trying to be in his league.

Back home she translated her "studies" into a passable picture of a jackrabbit sitting on its haunches under the maple tree. The fur was awful to draw, but she got on better with the ears and whiskers. But apparently not well enough.

"Something special, I said. Not to copy another student's work. Such lack of imagination! Such lack of talent!" Mrs. Machenko threw down her sketch.

"But I didn't copy it, honestly. I saw the rabbit in — " She caught herself in time. "In the park."

"This rabbit? This sentimental fuzz-ball with the shiny nose? Escaped from Walt Disney perhaps, yes? Where are the muscles? Where are the bones? No, it is no use. You had better go back to copying vases." Mrs. Machenko's voice deepened tragically, and she swept on to the next student.

Barbara sat in mortified silence, until she caught Stan grinning at her.

"Don't worry," he whispered. "It's just her style. Listen to her going on at Terry."

"I don't know what went wrong. I put down what I saw, honestly."

"Let's have a look. No, you didn't really. You've got the tree and the grass quite well, because you really looked at them." Stan stopped and frowned. "I can't figure out where you were when you drew this. There's nowhere in the park where the grass is left to grow long like this."

"It . . . it's somewhere else."

"Really. Where?"

"It's a secret," Barbara blurted out and then blushed. Boy, do I sound dumb!

Stan grinned. "I bet you just got it out of a book. If you did, you got it wrong. Look." He began to work lightly over her sketch. "The ears are taller. This isn't a cottontail like Peter Rabbit. It's a jackrabbit, which is actually a kind of hare. And the skull's not round, it's more egg-shaped. And the thigh muscle's got to be a lot bigger. Remember how it can jump."

Suddenly the rabbit was alive on the page.

"It isn't fair! Why can you do it so easily and I can't do it at all?"

"What about me in gym? How d'you think I feel falling off that darn bar all the time?"

"You're okay on the ropes," Barbara said consolingly.

"That's just shoulder muscle. There's nothing wrong with my muscles, just my b-balance and co-ordination. I don't know how you do it. I've seen you a couple of times, working out with the gym team. You're fantastic."

Barbara blushed again. "There's nothing to it, really. You just kind of relax and let your body work into what you've thought out ahead of time."

"Like drawing a rabbit?"

They both laughed — but quickly stopped as Mrs. Machenko spun round in a clatter of beads.

FIVE

On Monday Stan's hand was bandaged and in a sling. "Here, let me," Barb said at lunch time, after watching him struggle one-handedly. She unwrapped his sandwich for him. "It's bad enough fighting plastic when you've got two hands. What happened? Did you catch it in the lawn mower?"

She saw him half nod and hesitate. He looked for a second as if he was actually going to cry. "I'm sorry. None of my business," she said quickly. He went on looking miserable and she touched his hand gently. "Does it hurt that bad?"

He shook his head and suddenly began talking, the words tumbling out, like she'd never heard him talk before.

"It's . . . oh, everything, I guess. Not just my hand. Dad, and my brothers Dimitri and Josef. They're everything I'm not and Dad despises me. We were f-fixing up the house this summer. They'd run up and down ladders with loads of asphalt shingles while I, Stan the klutz, stood at the bottom with my stomach churning at the very thought of climbing up there. So Dad put me on to clearing up the junk on the ground, and my brothers got their jollies trying to hit me with the old shingles as they ripped them off."

"Your Dad let them do that?"

"He just told me to quit dreaming and jump a bit f-faster." Stan shrugged.

"I used to be sorry I didn't have brothers or sisters, but maybe I'm lucky."

"I thought it wasn't going to be so bad this year. Dimitri's gone to college on a football scholarship. If only Josef'd leave me alone I'd be okay. B-but he's always enjoyed b-bugging me. Now Dimitri's away I guess he wants to prove that he's b-boss. He's found out about my sketching, though I tried to keep it a secret. I just knew he and Dad would be on my case. That sketch of the rabbit I did for school — I was planning to give it to Mother for her birthday. But Josef had to go snooping around and tackled me at dinner time, right in front of Dad. Said 'Stan likes woman's work' just because I was helping Mom with the dishes and then . . ." He swallowed hard.

"Go on, Stan."

"He said, 'Stan was drawing bunny rabbits in school today.' Well, you can imagine my Dad. 'No son of mine's going to grow up to be a sissy.' So then I was twice as careful, jamming a chair back under the doorknob of my room when I was working. It worked out okay, till Saturday."

"When your hand . . . ?"

Stan nodded. "Dad had me cleaning up the yard,

cutting down corn stalks and digging up the cabbage roots. He'd made an incinerator out of an old oil drum and pierced holes in its sides for ventilation, to burn all the garden trash."

"I thought that was illegal."

"That never stopped Dad. Most of the neighbours won't talk to him. It's hard on Mom. I was scared someone would phone the police and complain, those burning cabbage stalks smelt so gross. The woman across the lane came out and tore her sheets off the line and took them into her house and slammed the door. But it didn't bother Dad. He just laughed. 'Silly old cow. Serve her right for doing her wash on a Saturday.'

" 'Isn't burning garbage in the city illegal?' I asked. 'So let her complain,' Dad said back. 'I've lived in this house and paid taxes on it for twenty-seven years, and I've been burning my refuse every fall since then. Hurry up with those corn stalks.' That's my dad."

Stan looked so miserable that Barbara could hardly bear it. "That's terrible. But go on, or lunch break'll be over before you've told me what happened to your hand."

"We finished the garden and Dad didn't have any complaints for once. I was on my way in when Josef came bursting out of the house. He was waving my sketchbook over his head like some kind of trophy. I'd hidden it under my mattress, so he must have been taking my room apart looking for something to bug me with. I tried to kick him, knee him, anything. I didn't care. He's taller than I am and about ten kilos heavier. He just held me off and laughed at me and tossed the sketchbook to my dad. That was worse than anything. His hands were filthy from working in the yard all day. He scuffed the pages over, dirt and fingermarks everywhere, and I yelled at him. 'What's this?' he said. 'For crying out loud! Birds? Flowers? My son drawing *flowers*. And more of those damn rabbits!' Then before I could do anything he flipped my book slap into the incinerator.''

"Your drawings! Stan, how awful!"

He gave a lopsided painful grin. "I got it back. I guess I was so mad and I wasn't thinking, or I couldn't have done it. I just about dived into that flaming oil drum and fished my book out. Dad didn't know what to do, he kept slapping at my right arm, where the sleeve of my shirt had caught. 'It's only a joke,' he kept saying. 'Can't you take a joke?' "

"Didn't it hurt like crazy?"

"I didn't really notice it at first. I ran for the house, up to my room. I began looking through my sketchbook. It was amazing—I guess it had fallen shut and I had reacted quickly—only the edges of a few pages were singed. The worst damage was Dad's filthy hands. It was then that I noticed that my right hand was really hurting. When I looked at it I nearly threw up. It was black, of course, they both were, but there was this enormous blister puffing up. My sleeve was black too, and the stuff turned to powder when I touched it. I had this bizarre idea that the same thing might happen if I touched my hand. I didn't try. By then it was hurting too much."

Barbara shivered. Nothing as awful had *ever* happened to her. She wondered what she would do if it did.

"Anyway," Stan went on, "Mom came in and saw my arm and she drove me to Emergency." He laughed. "It was very funny, really. My mom is so quiet, never talking back or pushy, but in less than five minutes she had me sitting in a treatment room with a doctor and a nurse cleaning up the mess. They gave me injections for the pain and against infection and splinted it up."

"Is it going to be okay? I mean, burns . . ."

"The doctor said he'd look at it in a couple of days, unless my temperature went up or there were any other problems. But it's okay, I guess. Then he turned to my Mom and said — ", Stan began to laugh. "He said, 'Mrs. Natyshyn, if I were you I'd confiscate that chemistry set until he's older and wiser!' I couldn't believe it. My mom *lying* about what had happened!"

"Why did she?" Barbara blurted, and then caught herself. "I'm sorry. I guess that's kind of personal."

"It's okay. I don't mind telling *you* somehow. I asked her that on the way home, and she just said, 'Stan, I had to tell him something and I wasn't going to expose my family's shame before strangers. That your father . . . that you . . . oh, Stan, love, how could you be so foolish?' Then she began crying and I felt just awful. But at the same time I knew that if it had happened all over again, I'd still probably risk getting burned to rescue my sketchbook. Dumb, eh?"

"No, Stan. Not dumb at all. Are your dad and brother any nicer to you now?"

"Like in a book? Dad and Josef truly repentant and reformed? Nah, it's not like that. They still think I'm a sissy, only now they know I'm a stupid sissy. D'you know what Dad said when Mom got me home? He said, 'Only a moron'd put his hand in a fire, for God's sake.' " Stan scrunched up his lunch bag and threw it at the garbage can.

"What did you mom say to *that*?"

"Mom never said a word, as far as I know. It worried me at first. Then I saw it from her point of view. Mom's an old-fashioned kind of person. I guess when she agreed to honour and obey when they got married, she really meant it. She just couldn't tell Dad that he was wrong, even when he was."

"That sounds weak, but the way you say it I don't think it is. I think your mom must be a very strong person underneath."

"She is that." The bell rang and they got to their feet. "Well, thanks for listening to me sound off."

"Wait, I want to know— Is your sketchbook all right?"

"You ask like it matters."

"Well, of course it does. It's what all this is about."

"Most of the sketches are okay. The thing that's bugging me is not having a private place to keep my things. And not having anywhere to go to sketch either. Dad's really on my case now. It's crazy, isn't it? If I was into football like Dimitri or Josef, nothing would be good enough for me. But because I want to be an artist, he acts like I'm some sort of pervert."

A private place. It was so evident. Barbara swallowed. But it was *hers*. What would happen if she shared it? Maybe the magic would go. Maybe he'd laugh at it and at her efforts to make it something more than it had been. But could she really enjoy Campbell's Bush now, knowing what it might mean to Stan? Darn, I wish this hadn't happened. I wish I hadn't asked him about his hand. I wish I hadn't got involved.

She took a deep breath. "Um, Stan, are you doing anything after school? If you're not, well, there's something I'd like to show you."

"Sure, I'm free. What's it all about?"

"It's . . . it's kind of secret. You won't tell?" Suppose he spreads it around. Suppose all the kids come along. Why did I . . . ?

"Hey, Barbara, it's all right. You don't have to if you don't want—"

"But I do. I think." She managed a weak laugh as they went back into class. "See you after school, okay?"

SIX

When Barbara got out of school that afternoon Stan was waiting for her. Part of her was pleased, but part of her wished he'd forgotten all about it. Suppose he laughed at Campbell's Bush? Suppose he thought it was dumb? Worst of all, suppose the magic disappeared once she shared it? Full of these worries, she scowled and muttered "Hi."

"C-can I c-carry your books?" he asked as they began to walk down the road.

"No, it's okay." She hugged them to her chest.

"You live in Westwood Acres, don't you?"

"Yeah. Crummy, isn't it?"

"Why would you say that? It looks pretty nice to me. I'd like to live this close to the park. Our house is about ten blocks north of here — it's a drag when I want to grab some time sketching."

"Here's our unit." Barbara stopped. "Great view, huh? Smiths's Tool and Die Works."

"Barbara, what's bugging you? If you've changed your mind and don't want to tell me your big secret, that's okay. I'd still like us to be friends, though."

She stared at the sidewalk, the corner of her math text digging painfully into her ribs. *Come on, Barbara*, she told herself. *You've got to take risks sometimes, or you'll never get anywhere.*

She made up her mind. "Okay. Dump your books in the hall. You can pick them up later. Now come on. This way." She caught his hand and dragged him across the street. "Only you've got to swear that you'll never tell a living soul about this place. Do you swear?"

"I do." He put his bandaged hand on his heart and looked dopey.

"I'm serious, Stan. May your feet rot off if you tell."

"That's a pretty fierce oath. All right. May my feet rot off if I tell. Now, where are we going? It looks most unpromising."

"You'll see." She led him along the gritty street, dodging blowing paper and garbage containers. "If you come here by yourself, you must remember to be really careful. Don't let anyone see you go in. If anyone's around, just walk another block and don't cut back till they've gone."

"See me go in where? Is this some kind of joke?"

Barbara giggled. "It's where I saw the rabbit. Right here. You'd never guess, would you?"

"A rabbit? You're having me on. Wrong park, Barb, this is the *industrial* one."

"You'll see. Now, is anyone looking? In here, quick."

"Ouch! What was that?" Stan tripped over a railway tie.

"Do be careful. If you break an ankle I'll have to get help and it'll ruin everything."

"Thanks, Florence Nightingale! Say, this is something else!"

Barbara ran lightly between the ties to the fence. "It's so wonderfully secret, isn't it? Through a hole in the wall, down the passage and . . . well, here we are." She couldn't keep the pride out of her voice. "Getting over's easy. You put your right foot *here*. And your left foot against the fence. Then grab the top and you're — Oh, I forgot your burnt hand. Maybe I'd better give you a boost."

She linked her hands and Stan put his foot in them and shot upward. The fence shook and he vanished. There came the sound of tearing cloth and then silence.

"Are you all right?"

"Fine. Just my windbreaker . . . Oh, wow!"

His voice said it all. It was all right. Barbara felt a warm glow of relief and happiness. Her choice had been the right one. The only thing Campbell's Bush had lacked was someone to share it with. She vaulted lightly over the fence. Stan hadn't blundered around or trampled through the long grass that she had left undisturbed for the rabbit to hide in. He was standing with his back to the fence, just looking.

"Well, here it is." Her voice wobbled unexpectedly. She waved her arm around. "As you can see, this is an aspen. Over there are two maples. They come with the place. The rest I mostly did myself during the summer. I know it's not much, but I had practically no allowance and I had to scrounge. That old Coleman cooler, I got it at a garage sale for three dollars. Nearly killed me getting it over the fence, but it's great for chocolate bars and potato chips. I found a cushion in a plastic cover and I keep a garbage bag under it for when the ground's damp."

"I love the pool, the way it reflects the sky. It makes the whole place seem bigger."

"I thought that the first time I came here. I was determined to have a pool, but it was horribly difficult. The ground was too hard to dig properly and I only had a little garden trowel. I had to scrape away the weeds and grass and as much dirt as I could from the lowest spot and then spread a sheet of plastic across the hollow and edge it with bits of broken brick and stone. There was lots of rubble in the grass, enough to make a pretty neat edging and hold the plastic firm. It was wonderful after the first rain. I climbed the fence into the garden and there was the sky, a splash of blue reflected in my new pool. It was perfect!" She smiled at the memory.

"Anyway, I began spending my leftover money on peanuts for the blue jays, but the squirrels must have sent out signals to all their friends to come and steal them, and they ate the lot the day I put them out and the blue jays didn't even get to taste them."

"Was that when you built the birdfeeder and the purple martins' house?"

"Yes, I wanted something decent for the small birds, but I had an awful time. There was nowhere at home where I could cut up wood, and Mom didn't have any tools except a screwdriver. I scrounged around the lumber yard and got a purple martin house and a bird table, all ready to assemble. They were only just a bit damaged and they were on at half price. What do you think?"

She looked around. To her the secret garden was

58

perfect. The pool shone. The bird table hung, a little crookedly, from the bough of the maple, and the martin house stood on a post.

"There aren't any martins yet," she apologized.

"I bet they'll be along in the spring. Once they've had a chance to talk it over with their aunts and uncles and cousins."

"That's *exactly* what I thought. Isn't it wonderful to think that in the spring this garden will still be here, with the flowers growing and the birds coming back?" She could feel the smile spread across her face. She was grinning like an idiot and she couldn't help it. It really was going to be all right. Stan was the perfect companion for Campbell's Bush. "I hang up the peanuts for the blue jays now. Otherwise the squirrels steal them all. They must sneak over the roofs."

"There's probably a special squirrel highway up there with traffic control and everything."

She laughed. "Over here is where I sit most of the time. The sun just soaks into the concrete. And the cooler's practically hidden in the long grass. Have a chocolate bar? I keep a selection of food here against an attack of the galloping munchies."

"It's great. Fabulous. Here we are, sitting in the sun and no one knows — " He stopped suddenly as he spotted the double doors.

"You've got good eyes," Barb said. "I didn't notice the doors for ages. Well, you only do when the sun's getting low and the crack in the door casts a shadow that particular way. But it's all right." Barbara explained about the office with the poster of Copenhagen Harbour on the other side of the double doors.

He laughed. "It's more fun knowing that's going on and nobody there knows about this place. It really *is* your place, isn't it? Does it have a name?"

"Of course. Campbell's Bush."

"Is Campbell someone special?"

"I'll show you on the way out. It's obvious when you see it. I wish you'd seen the garden before that frost. There were masses of flowers and birds. D'you know, the other day I noticed a mountain ash sapling poking out above the long grass over there. Imagine. In a few years that'll be a real tree with berries. Then maybe the waxwings will come here too."

"And I'll get a chance to draw them properly. That is . . . if you let me come again."

"Of course I will, Stan. That's what I meant. It's yours now as well. It's ours."

"Th-that's f-fantastic. The best present I ever had. Thanks, Barbara."

They sat munching their chocolate bars until the sun dropped behind the western warehouse and a chilly breeze sprang up.

"Time to go. And mounds of homework to do."

"We could bring it here on warm days, maybe. And keep extra sweaters tucked away in the cooler."

"Great idea."

They climbed the fence and walked in single file along the dark passage. "I always check around the corner," Barbara whispered. "Just to make sure no one's in sight. Though no one ever is. It's all trucks and stuff and they pay no attention. All clear."

Out on 113th Avenue she pointed at the warehouse above them. Stan's eyes followed her finger.

"Hodgson and Campbell and Sons Ltd.? Oh, I get it. Ha! I love it! Our own piece of real estate with the name above the gate."

When they met in the school lunchroom next day Stan showed Barbara a new sketchbook. It was a real beauty, with a linen cover and an elastic band to clip around and keep it closed.

"It's gorgeous. It must have cost a fortune."

"Mom slipped it to me last night. 'You just fill it up, son,' she said to me. Then she went back to cooking dinner with a look on her face like she'd done something wicked. If you don't mind I'll leave it in the cooler at Campbell's Bush. Safer than at home."

"Of course. Great idea. Then nosy Josef won't get his hands on it. Maybe cover it with a plastic bag, though I think the cooler's watertight."

She was eating peanut butter sandwiches again.

"You must like that stuff a lot."

"This? It's cheap, that's all. Better than sardines, anyway."

"I can't figure you out, Barbara Coutts. You've got all those designer jeans and shirts and stuff, but you're living in a low-rental townhouse and you eat peanut butter sandwiches all the time."

"The clothes are just leftovers," Barbara explained. "In another six months I won't be able to get into any of them. We had lots of money when Dad lived with us, but now we don't, okay?"

Stan nodded. "The funny thing is your clothes kind of put me off you at first. I thought you were a snob. But you're not a bit."

"Well, thanks." She laughed. "Actually I think I was. I was in a foul mood when we moved. But Campbell's Bush helped a lot. And having you for a friend."

"It's made a heck of difference to me too. The funny thing is I don't seem to care about Josef's snide remarks anymore. They just roll off me, where before I used to get really mad, you know. So now Josef comes off like an idiot, going on at me and me not paying any attention. Just wish I'd thought of that before!"

During the next week they went to the garden every afternoon as soon as school was over, except on gym days, when Stan went by himself. Once there they talked and talked. They did their homework and Stan sketched. But there was never enough time. It seemed that they had hardly got settled before they had to go home for their suppers.

Barbara found the most difficult thing was keeping Campbell's Bush a secret from her mother.

"Where were you?"

"Doing homework with Stan."

"At his house? You'd better leave the phone number with me. And I hope you're not a nuisance to —"

"It's okay, Mom. We study in the park anyway, not at Stan's house." Well, it is, sort of, she told herself, crossing her fingers in her lap.

"Don't get chilled. The evenings are getting shorter and shorter. It'll be winter soon."

"Don't, Mom." Barbara shivered.

"I thought you loved winter."

"I guess I'm changing. Maybe it's part of growing up."

"I just hate the thought of it getting too cold for Campbell's Bush," she said to Stan after school next day. "I think I'd go crazy if I didn't have this place."

"It's an escape, isn't it? Like the jackrabbit, having a place to run to that's real, not just mowed grass and trim bushes and kids playing baseball."

"A place to calm down, too. Sometimes Mom makes me so mad, and I don't really know why. She's not doing anything, just being there. But I want to scream. I know I'm not being fair to her, but I just can't help it."

"Maybe it's because she's there and your father isn't."

Barbara stared at him. "That doesn't ... Well, maybe you're right. Anyway, I've got this crazy idea of building a little house — well, more of a lean-to, I guess. But I don't know how and I haven't any tools or anything."

"My father's got a big workshop. I can borrow some tools and we could do all the work out here."

"Really? Could you do that without him noticing — or Josef? It would be fantastic if you could. What I thought of was a simple design with a sloping roof down from the loading bay to shed the rain, and a side wall on the north side. We wouldn't need more if we built it in the corner here. And the front would be open, of course, without a wall at all."

"Like this?" Stan made a neat sketch on the corner of his page.

"That's it exactly. Perfect. It'd be great if we could have a bit of plywood for a floor."

"And why not a piece of leftover carpet on top of that?"

"Yes. Indoor-outdoor carpet, so it won't rot."

"We could do the roof and sides in shingles," Stan said. "It'd blend better into the garden. We don't want something that looks like a tacky shed, do we?"

"Fantastic! Only . . ."

"What's wrong?"

"I don't have any money for all this stuff."

"Not to worry. I bet we can scrounge most of it from the throw-out bin at the lumber yard, and Dad has bits left over from renovating the house. I can certainly get plywood for the floor and sheathing for the roof. I'll work out what we'll need over the next few days, and then maybe we can work on it over next weekend."

Our own secret house, Barbara thought as she dried the supper dishes. Somewhere totally secret and safe, a place to hold inside herself when things were rotten, like in art class or social studies, or when she suddenly missed Dad so much it hurt . . .

"You look all lit up and excited, Barb. Anything I should know about?"

"Nope. How about you, Mom? What are you slaving on over your hot typewriter these days?"

"Well, thanks for asking." Her mother laughed, taking the sting out of her words. "I have some short stories doing the rounds. And I'm very busy on the prison reform article. Been out to the jail interviewing prisoners. Thank goodness the TV series is just about finished."

"What's it about?"

"Alberta's economy: signposts to prosperity."

Barbara pulled a face. "Ugh, boring stuff!"

"Not at all. Actually it's fascinating. Little bits and pieces like a jigsaw puzzle, that all come together to give you a clear picture. For instance, I just got hold of a strong rumour that someone from Hong Kong is going to take over that area across the road — Westwood Industrial Park. That they're going to tear down those rundown warehouses and build a big electronics manufacturing complex. Well, imagine what *that* would do to the local economy. . . . Barbara, what on earth's the matter with you? You look as if you've seen a ghost!"

"I'm . . . just fine. You're right, Mom, it's fascinating. Why, maybe I won't have to stare out of my bedroom window at Smith's Tool and Die Works much longer. How about that?"

"Don't hold your breath. It may turn out to be just that — a rumour. But that's the kind of interesting thing I dig up when I'm —"

"Mom, would you excuse me. I just remembered there's someone I've got to talk to . . . homework . . . okay? I won't be long." She slid out the front door and ran all the way to Stan's house.

She hesitated outside. She didn't really want to have to meet his father or that rotten brother. But this was urgent. She squared her shoulders and pushed the doorbell.

Luckily it was Stan who answered. "Barb, what are *you* doing here?"

"I'm sorry," she whispered, "I've got to see you. It's absolutely vital. Can you walk down the road with me?"

As soon as they reached the sidewalk she told him what her mother had just said. "They could pull it down any time. Any time at all! Isn't it awful?"

"Are you sure about this? Your mother *did* say it was only a rumour? Maybe it'll never happen."

"With my luck it will. Stan, if anything were to happen to Campbell's Bush I just couldn't bear it. I don't know

65

what I'd do. Run away maybe. Go to Toronto and find Dad."

"You're crazy, you know that?" Stan ran his hand through his hair. "Look, it's no good going off in all directions. What we've got to do is to find out if this rumour's true."

"How?"

"Well, you could ask your mother to dig a bit further, couldn't you?"

"I don't think so." Barbara sighed. "She said the series was pretty well wrapped up. She's working on this dumb prison thing now. I can't believe it. All our plans for a little house of our own. . . ."

"We'll go right ahead with them, that's what we'll do. We can't stop planning just because something bad *might* happen tomorrow. It won't anyway. I bet even if the property *is* sold it'll take forever before anything is actually done. Come on, cheer up! On Friday you can help me haul stuff over to Campbell's Bush and we'll start building. We won't let any old rumour spoil our special place."

Late on Friday evening Barbara waited under the light at the corner of Stan's street.

"Sorry I'm late," he panted. "I had to wait till Dad and Josef were safely into pro football in front of the TV. I got some great plywood that Dad didn't use because of the knots, and some roof sheathing just a bit spoiled. They're murder to carry. Grab hold quick."

With two of them the load was manageable, and they made a second trip for a big bundle of two-by-twos.

"Whew! That's it," gasped Barbara as they heaved the second load over the fence.

"I'll be here first thing in the morning with hammers and nails and a saw," Stan promised.

"I'll join you just as soon as I can. I may have to bargain with Mom to get away before housecleaning, but I'll manage something."

Saturday morning was blustery, with a southwest wind that tore the clouds to shreds and set flags and banners cracking. It couldn't have been a better day from their point of view, since no one could possibly hear Stan's saw or the noise of hammering, even if anyone *had* been listening on the other side of one of the flat-faced warehouses.

Stan measured off the lengths of framing pieces on the two-by-twos and set Barbara to cutting them. By lunch time they had hammered together the frame, floored it and put on a plywood siding and a sheathing roof.

They took a quick break to gobble down a sandwich and then went scrounging at the lumber yard. They had to pay full price for a piece of plastic to cover the sheathing on the roof, but they got a special buy on some leftover bundles of shingles.

"I'll pay you back my share," panted Barbara as they lugged their new supplies back to the garden. "Just as soon as Mom can spare me some more allowance."

"Forget it. You going shares in Campbell's Bush balances it out."

"But . . ."

"Think how much it would cost me to pay you for half this land, with the prices of real estate being what they are."

"Prime real estate at that! Okay, Stan. Thanks."

All afternoon they hammered shingles onto the roof and down the north wall. They came back on Sunday afternoon to finish the job. It was perfect. The soft grey of the shingles blended into the concrete wall behind, while in front the grass grew untrampled to the little pool and the maples.

Barbara licked the blisters on her palms. "It's wonderful. But I'm glad I don't have to build houses for a living. Gosh, look at the time! I must run. I'm so far behind on my chores it's scary! See you!"

"I've hardly seen you recently," her mother remarked when she got home. "I hope that means that you're having fun and not that you're getting into mischief."

"Fun definitely. Mom, are you lonely or something?" She felt suddenly guilty. It couldn't be much fun for Mom, sitting at the typewriter all week, with no one to talk to on weekends. And she, Barbara, had been kind of rotten so many times. "Would you like to play Scrabble this evening? Or Monopoly," she added hopefully, since even if Mom only drew six tiles a time she could usually skunk her at Scrabble. At Monopoly she had a fighting chance.

"Actually, I thought for a treat we might go out for supper. Nothing extravagant, just fried chicken or ribs."

"Lovely. I'll get the vacuuming done and then get changed."

"Make sure you brush that stuff out of your hair. What on earth is it? It looks like sawdust."

"I've been helping Stan do some carpentry work," Barbara said.

It was best to tell the truth, she thought as she cleaned up the house, but she would have to be careful, more careful than Stan, whose family didn't seem to care very much about what he was up to. Whereas Mom was liable to weasel her secret out of her with plain ordinary motherly curiosity.

Once they were in the restaurant and had ordered, Barbara quickly put the conversation on a safe course. "How's the series on the economy doing?"

"All finished and sent off. Next month's groceries are safely taken care of. No caviar, I'm afraid. Still macaroni cheese and peanut butter, but we won't starve."

"I hate caviar anyway, yucky. . . . Mom, what was that rumour about some millionaire buying the industrial park?"

"What about it?"

"Is it *true*?"

"My dear, I don't have the least idea. All sorts of rumours fly around about real estate and the money market. If I knew which ones were really true we wouldn't be eating macaroni and peanut butter so often. Anyway, why all this sudden interest in my work? I don't remember you getting excited about it before."

Barbara blushed. "Don't remind me. I was a selfish brat, but give me a chance. I'm growing up, really I am. Tell me what else you're working on," she added hastily. If Mom suspected that she was only interested in Westwood Industrial Park she might start wondering exactly *where* Stan and she did their homework.

"Let me see. I have a contract for a TV series on the future of Alberta's natural resources. And then there's that article I told you about on the penal system on the prairies."

"Prisons and stuff? I remember. Are you really going out there to talk to them?"

"Sure. And interview lawyers and prisoners' advocates

and so on. It's very interesting. Tell me, Barb, what do *you* think about people being put in prison for their crimes?"

"I think it's really mean, practically out of the middle ages. We ought to be able to educate people to behave properly."

"What if they refuse?"

"You could make them . . ."

"Like the hero of *Clockwork Orange*?"

"That scary movie, you mean? Changing their brains, so they have no free will? I guess that'd be worse than prison, wouldn't it. And then there are mass murderers. It's pretty confusing, isn't it? I'd like to read the article when you're done and find out what *you* think."

"I'm having a lot of difficulty making up my own mind. Talking to the prisoners . . . Some of them had such rotten childhoods that in a way it's not surprising they went off the rails. Don't misunderstand, Barb. I have no sympathy with violence, but when I see a woman who's been a victim of violence all her life, I can understand how she might come to batter her own child. Or a man murder his own mother after a lifetime of physical and psychological abuse." She shivered suddenly. "*He* was a strange one."

"*Who?*"

"Jack Norton. Murdered his mother and— But, my goodness, what on earth am I doing talking about such sordid things? This is a celebration. Have you room for dessert after all that chicken and ribs?"

"Have I? Mom, what a dumb question!"

Stan phoned Barbara just after she got home. "Could you come to supper with me tomorrow evening?"

70

"That's very kind" Barbara hesitated, trying to think of a not too untruthful excuse to get out of the invitation. She hadn't been inside the Natyshyn home, and she was pretty sure she didn't want to. "I should ask my mom."

She could hear Stan's laugh. "You do that. Oh, it won't be at my place. Somewhere else. A surprise."

"I didn't mean . . . well, okay. Thanks, I'd love to."

"Meet me at Campbell's Bush at six o'clock, okay?"

"That's a funny place to . . . all right. I'll be there."

She wondered after she had put the phone down if she was supposed to wear something special, but if she were going to have to climb the fence Stan wouldn't expect her to wear a dress. She settled for a pair of her old designer jeans, getting horribly tight this year, and a sweater. Promptly at six o'clock she climbed the fence into Campbell's Bush.

The first thing she noticed was the delicious smell of outdoor cooking. Then Stan came out of the lean-to and bowed.

"Welcome to Chez Campbell."

"How have you . . . ? You've got a camp stove. Fantastic!"

"Pray be seated, madam."

She sat on the cushion he indicated and watched as he expertly fried onion rings and flipped over hamburgers. "I'd like to have made french fries, but I think they're beyond a Coleman, so I settled for hash browns. Here. Hold the plate. Go ahead. Eat it while it's hot. Is it okay?"

"Great," she said with her mouth full. "Is there a special reason for this celebration, or did you just feel in the mood?"

"It's exactly a week since you introduced me to Campbell's Bush and I wanted to thank you. And celebrate finishing the lean-to. So I bought the Coleman stove. It can stay here with the cooler. I thought it'd be useful now the weather's getting cold. We can have hot soup when we feel like it and beans and stew on Saturdays."

"Stan, you're great. I'm so glad I asked you. It'd be nothing without you. Now it's like having a real home, a place of our own. I haven't missed Willow Heights once since you've been part of the secret garden."

And I've hardly thought about Dad either, she realized with a shock. She hadn't even missed him when she dusted his photograph on Saturday.

"It's the same for me, Barb. It's weird what a difference it's made. Josef doesn't bug me anymore. If he wants to snoop in my room, let him. I don't care. I've got all the peace and quiet I want here. And I've had a great idea. I'm going to fill my new book with sketches of Campbell's Bush. Then when it's filled I'll show them to Mrs. Machenko. It'll be like the portfolio an artist collects to help him get a job."

"You're going to get a job?"

"No, I'm not good enough yet. Advice is what I need. I've just got to convince my family that I'm serious about art. I expect Mrs. Machenko can tell me about competitions or scholarships or things like that. If I won something or had money towards my art education, then I think Dad might be more reasonable. Football scholarships he understands, so maybe I can make him understand an art school one. If I should get so lucky."

SEVEN

It was one of those awful classes, like Show and Tell, but thank goodness this only happened once a year. It was called Career Choices, which sounded innocent enough; but you had to watch out, thought Barbara, or, like Show and Tell, it left you wide open to any enemies you might have — that is, if you were stupid enough to expose your secret desires to the whole class. So most of the girls said things like "I guess I'll work in an office" or "I'll go in for nursing" even if their ambition was really to drive one of the monster trucks up at the Tar Sands or be a botanist on the Upper Amazon.

Barbara was afraid that Stan might make a fool of himself — after all, everyone knew he could draw — but it was all right. "Guess I'll go on to university, maybe be an engineer," he mumbled in a bored tone.

Then up piped Terry Roberts in his silly squeaky voice. "I'm going to be a chartered accountant like my dad. He works in the City Planning Department deciding what's going to be built where."

Barbara turned to stare at him and saw Stan's head pivot at the exact same moment on the same invisible string. At lunch time they got Terry in a corner by himself, which wasn't difficult. He usually ate alone.

"What's all this about your dad working in City Planning? Does he know what changes are going to be made?"

"Like what?"

"Like maybe in Westwood Industrial Park?"

Terry took an enormous bite out of his sandwich and nodded vigorously. "That's his job," he said indistinctly, looking up at Stan and ignoring Barbara, who sat on his other side. "Why?"

"I've got a job for you, young Terry. Something special and secret."

Terry nodded, his eyes larger than usual behind his thick lenses.

"We need you to find out if it's true that some millionaire's going to buy Westwood Industrial Park and tear down all the old warehouses and build an electronics factory."

Terry nodded again.

"You'll do it? And not let on to anyone else?"

"Like —" Terry swallowed. "Like in the secret service?"

"Yeah, I guess so. Like the secret service."

"I'll do it, Stan. I won't let you down." He walked off, his face shining, his chest puffed out.

"Do you really think *he* can find anything out?" Barbara looked after him doubtfully.

"I'll bet on it. Funny little guy, isn't he? Sometimes I wonder what's really going on in his head."

In fact Terry was floating on air. His wildest dream had just been realized. For Terry had a secret life. Until Grade Seven his chief happiness had been reading adventure stories. He had read the adventures of both Sherlock Holmes and the Scarlet Pimpernel. He had devoured the Three Musketeers and the Count of Monte Cristo, the stories of King Arthur and of Beau Geste. In his dreams he forgot the unkind world of school, where to be small, fat and as short-sighted as a bat was to be ignored or mercilessly baited. In his dreams he was as tall and good-looking as Stan Natyshyn, as brilliantly deductive as Sherlock Holmes and as brave as the Scarlet Pimpernel.

Though Stan didn't remember, they had met once before when he was in Grade Five and Terry was in Grade Four. A gang of boys had grabbed his glasses right off his face and then played a kind of Blind Man's Bluff with him, pinching him, spinning him around until he was dizzy and then challenging him to go for the pincher. It was Stan who had got his glasses back for him and sent his tormentors flying.

Terry had been accelerated into Grade Seven, and he sat right next to Stan in class. Now he dared to go one step further and include a fictional Stan in his daydreams. He was rereading *A Tale of Two Cities*, revelling in the excitement of the story. Slowly, almost without his meaning it, the hero, Charles Darnay, began to take on the appearance of Stan, tall, wide-shouldered and dark, while he, Terry Roberts, cast aside his glasses and stepped boldly into the role of the dissolute Sydney Carton, who would, for the love of Darnay's wife, Lucie, take Darnay's place at the guillotine.

"It is a far, far better thing that I do than I have ever done." Terry shivered in anticipation of the glorious ending and curled up into the prickly comfort of the sofa. As he read his nose sank closer and closer to the page.

Now, on a Monday morning, in the third week of September, Terry left for school eagerly. It was thrilling to sit next to his hero, anticipating the evening's chapter, knowing ahead of time the supreme sacrifice that he, Terry Roberts, alias Sydney Carton, was to make. It was a pity that the drippy new girl, Barbara, who sat on the other side of Stan, was skinny and had braces, quite unlike the bewitching Lucie.

He glanced at Stan and saw, with concern, that his right hand was heavily bandaged and in a sling. Probably hurt rescuing some other kid from a gang, he thought, and wondered how to fit the injury into his daydreams. Perhaps Stan had been injured when he was thrown into the Bastille . . .

"Terry, are you paying attention?"

He jumped. "Yes, Mrs. Duvall."

"Can you see the board properly from back there? You may come up to the front row if you like."

Terry, who had sat in the front row of every classroom since Grade One, shook his head dumbly and clung to the edges of his desk. Leanne, who sat behind him, giggled and poked her friend Patty and whispered to her.

At lunch they pounced on him. "You're in love with Stan Natyshyn. Goofy Stan and Bobby the Book-worm!"

"Four Eyes and the Klutz. A perfect match!"

It was agony and joy. He wanted to boast about his hero, but he knew he had to keep his other life secret or he was dead. He bolted for the washroom where the tormenting girls couldn't follow him and ate his meat pie and apple behind the locked door of one of the cubicles.

When he ventured out he saw Stan and Barbara, heads together, talking earnestly. He sighed and regretfully cast Barbara, braces and all, as Lucie Darnay.

Today was Career Choices Day at school. Terry looked forward mildly to sharing his ambitions with the other students, but nothing had prepared him for the incredible conversation with Stan that had followed. To discover the truth about Westwood Industrial Park, and to do it secretly! But why? The mystery devoured him. He could think of nothing else. Terry Roberts, superspy. He could hardly wait to talk to his father.

That night at the dinner table, Terry wriggled in his chair. "Would *you* know if Westwood Industrial Park was going to be pulled down and redeveloped?" He asked in a rush.

Mr. Roberts stared at his son. "What on earth made you ask *that* particular question? About Westwood in particular?"

Oh, dear. Now what had he done? It would have been better, thought Terry frantically, if he could have rifled his father's briefcase and secretly photographed the plans. Except that he knew the briefcase was empty — his father never brought work home.

Mr. Roberts was still staring at him. "It . . . it came up in school," Terry managed to say. "Career Choices Day today. Remember, I told you."

His father looked puzzled. "Yes, but what has that to do with — "

"It *is* just a rumour then, isn't it? It's not true that a millionaire is going to turn the park into an electronics factory?"

"I don't know where you got your information, son, and I won't press you to tell me. But I must warn you *not* to repeat it." His father's lips closed in a thin line. He got up from the table without waiting for dessert and retired to the living room, leaving Terry to stare after him in dismay.

Next day Terry sought out Stan when that creepy Barbara wasn't around. "My father won't tell me anything," he said importantly. "But he was furious and didn't even have dessert, so that must mean the rumour's true, musn't it?"

"Thanks, Terry," was all Stan said, but Terry noticed that he looked worried. Why should it matter to him what was going on in Westwood Industrial Park? Terry made up his mind. Whatever it was, Stan was in trouble. Something about the Industrial Park that he'd sworn not to tell. It was clear to Terry what he must do. He must follow Stan everywhere and guard his back. Secretly. As any good spy would do for his friend.

"Terry Roberts has been acting really weird ever since I asked him to find about the industrial park," Stan remarked.

"Weird how?"

"Ouch, watch that cocoa — it's flaming hot. Well, he's been following me around. Not obviously. Sort of sneakily. He's getting pretty difficult to throw off. I had to dodge around the block before I dared come in to Campbell's Bush this evening. Imagine if he found out about this . . ."

"He musn't. Terry Roberts! It would ruin it all."

Barbara looked lovingly around their domain. Campbell's Bush was like a golden square dropped down in the grey grottiness of the industrial park. It was in the glory of Indian summer, the sky intensely blue, the sun boiling hot out of the wind, which didn't touch them in their cosy lean-to. They had made it well. They'd lain a piece of shag carpet on the floor, and there were extra sweaters if they needed them.

At this moment the western sky was aflame, the last leaves hung like shreds of beaten gold from the aspen and the ground beneath the maples was bright with red and orange. Half a dozen chickadees called *dee, dee, dee* from the trees. A small plane chugged overhead. The quietness flooded in behind its passing.

Barbara sighed. "I just can't bear to think of bulldozers coming in and tearing it apart. Stan, isn't there anything else we can do?"

"Not as long as it's in the secret planning stage. I mean, everybody'd just deny it if we made a fuss. And of course," he added thoughtfully, "if we *do* make a fuss, that's the end of Campbell's Bush as our special private place."

"We're caught both ways, then. We're helpless."

"Cheer up, Barb. It might come to nothing. You know these international real estate deals. Half the time nothing happens or they go somewhere else. Can you get your mother to scrounge for more information?"

"I don't think so. She's working on the prison article now. Interviewing convicts, even taking their photographs. I think it's kind of spooky."

She sipped her cocoa. "Bad enough worrying about City Planning. More to the point, it'd be a disaster if Terry found out about Campbell's Bush. You're absolutely right, Stan. We're going to have to think of something to put him off you."

The sun was setting and, in the shadows on the other side of the fence, Terry shivered in the wind that suddenly cut like a knife down the narrow passage from 113th Avenue, but he paid no attention to his discomfort. When he sat sideways, with his right eye to the crack in the fence, he could see between clumps of grass clear across the garden to the house they had built on the far side. He could see their faces and hands and the steam rising in clouds from their mugs. He longed to be there, sharing whatever they were drinking. Sharing their secret.

But it was *theirs*. In imagining that Terry would blab it all over school Barbara was doing him a grievous wrong. If the Grade Nine boys were to sit on his legs and pull out his fingernails one by one with red-hot pincers, he would never divulge the existence, much less the whereabouts, of their secret garden. It was Stan Natyshyn's secret and his alone.

He thought with a real pang that it would be so much nicer if Stan had shared the secret with *him*, instead of with Barbara Coutts. But Terry was so accustomed to the role of second best that the pang was only momentary. It was replaced with a great sense of responsibility.

Terry now felt like a fellow spy, keeping a sleepless watch upon the gate of the garden, lest their enemies surprise them while they dallied within, drinking hot soup or cocoa. The problem of getting out of sight, when they decided to leave, had exercised his mind. But he found that the warehouse on 113th Avenue, to the west of the passage to the secret garden, had a recessed doorway, deep enough for him to hide in until they emerged from the garden and turned east towards home.

This was now his second evening's watch. He knew that his mother was bound to be a little testy when he did not come straight home from school as he used to, but after all he *was* in Junior High now. He would tell her, straight out, that he was helping his friend Stan. Mother would understand. Even if she were difficult, he would have to be firm. He was sure that mothers never got in the way of a spy's solemn duty.

As he sat in the shadows, slowly freezing in the north wind, he felt a warm glow inside. He deeply approved of the secret garden, with its shingled house in the corner and the dark and gloomy passage leading to it. It was something that he wished he had invented himself.

EIGHT

"Thanksgiving on Monday." Barbara slammed her math book shut. It was Saturday afternoon. "There. That's the end of it. Two days without homework, yeah!"

"That's something to be thankful for, I guess."

"I've got so much to give thanks for. It's hard to believe that just three months ago I was in deep despair. Now there's Campbell's Bush. Having you as a best friend. And the gym team. Preliminary trials in Calgary. Alison and Jessica and *me*. I still have to pinch myself."

"Hmm." Stan worked on a tricky bit of shading.

Barbara smiled. She had grown to enjoy Stan's silence. It was as much a part of Campbell's Bush as the maples and the reflecting pool. It was all a part of her now. Sometimes, when Mrs. Duvall got difficult over irregular verbs or when she was centering her concentration at the start of a difficult gym routine, she could reach inside herself and grab hold of the silence.

There was only one major problem in life. Dad.

"It's my birthday on Saturday, the day after the gym trials. I keep worrying: will Dad remember it? Remember *me?*"

Stan looked up from his work. "Any reason why he shouldn't?"

"Well, he hasn't written or phoned once since he left. I don't know where he is. Or how he is. Nothing."

"Does he ever write to your mom?"

Barbara shook her head and sighed. "It's . . . difficult. I can't talk to her about Dad. And I'm always in school when the mail comes, so I don't even know if she's heard from him. All I know is that she still gets lawyers' letters and sometimes some money."

"Did he ever forget your birthday before?"

"No. But Mom was there to remind him," she added honestly. "And his secretary. I know his secretary used to send flowers to Mom on her birthday and their anniversary, because once the bill came to the house by mistake instead of to the office. It said 'Ordered by Brenda Smith.' Mom was furious."

"I'll bet." He held his book out in front of him, looking critically at the sketch, his head tilted.

"May I look?" She took the book from him and leafed through it. It was almost full of sketches of chickadees and blue jays, of seagulls and squirrels, and — "There's a new one of our rabbit! It's ages since I've seen him. You are lucky! I just don't have enough time for Campbell's Bush right now, what with extra classes with Mrs. Rawlings, and I miss it a lot. But the rabbit's wonderful, he's so alive. You're getting really good, aren't you?"

"Yes, I think so. Being able to work in peace and quiet has made all the difference — well, almost quiet." He grinned at her and she stuck her tongue out.

"You've nearly finished the book. Only three pages left. Then you'll have to show it to Mrs. Machenko."

"If I can get up the nerve."

"You've *got* to, Stan. I'll nag you till you do. . . . It's wonderful to sit in the sun and forget about school and gym routines for a bit." She stretched and relaxed.

It would be so marvellous if she could find a way of asking Dad to come home for her birthday. Seeing him would be better than a million presents, better even than her own TV. Jessica had been given a portable TV for *her* last birthday, and she'd had a moment's hope that just maybe Dad would . . .

She looked at her watch. Five o'clock. She had helped Mom clean house and buy groceries in the morning and left her sitting at the table with her notes and typewriter. I hope she's finished, so I don't have to make supper, she thought.

"I have to go. Will you be here tomorrow? And Monday?"

"Not sure." He was shading a corner of his drawing with fine neat lines, his tongue between his teeth.

"Don't get cold. It's clouding over."

"Thank you, Gramma. I've got my Cowichan sweater stashed in the cooler if I get chilly."

"Well, Happy Thanksgiving. See you Tuesday." Barbara put a foot on the bottom fence cross piece and then stopped. "The rabbit isn't around today, is it?"

"Don't think so. Why?"

"Thought I heard a scuffling sound close by. I'd hate to

jump on the poor thing by mistake."

"D'you think it'd wait around for a great lump like you to jump on it?"

"Great *lump*? Just listen to who's talking!" She vaulted neatly over the fence just as Terry scuttled out of sight at the end of the passage.

I really will talk to Mom about my birthday, she decided as she walked briskly home, her breath puffing up in white clouds like a mini steam engine. If she's got Dad's phone number maybe she'll let me phone him and ask him to fly out for next Saturday. He could stay for the whole weekend . . .

As Barbara opened the front door the smell of stew on the edge of burning drifted out to meet her. She leapt for the kitchen and snatched the saucepan from the burner.

"Is that you, Barb?"

"No, it's the Great Pumpkin. Mom, you could have burned the house down!"

"Heavens, the dinner! I remember now, I opened a can and shoved it on the burner." Mom ran her hands through her hair. "I can't make up my mind which of these pictures to use in my article. Come and look. You might find them interesting."

The table was covered with glossy black-and-white photographs of men and women. "Not very glamorous, are they? Are *these* the criminals you've been interviewing?" The quite ordinary faces suddenly took on an aura of danger. Barbara scanned the pictures. "This woman's quite good-looking. And this guy, he's really handsome, isn't he?"

"Which one? Oh, him. He's Robert Lusaky. He killed his drug supplier in a fight."

Barbara shivered and put the pictures down quickly. "Weren't you scared?"

"Oddly enough, I wasn't. I found I was seeing them as human beings, like you and me, but ones who had made wrong decisions in life, for some reason or another. There was only one who gave me the shivers, and I'm not sure why. Him. Jack Norton. He murdered his mother and her boyfriend in a blind rage."

"Mom, weren't you scared to *death*?"

Her mother laughed. "Well, there *was* a guard in the room the whole time I was doing the interviews."

Barbara shuffled the photographs. "A murderer? He doesn't look like it, does he? He's got the sort of face you'd never notice in a crowd. I wonder what he was like as a kid. Can you tell anything from people's faces, do you suppose? Stan might know. I'd love Stan to see these. Could he?"

"So long as it's before the end of the long weekend. I'll be parcelling up the manuscript and the pictures to send out first thing Tuesday morning."

"I'll ask him to drop by tomorrow, okay? It'd be neat if he could guess who did what."

"It'd be remarkable. Those theories linking crime and facial characteristics are terribly outdated."

"That's me. Outdated before my time. Anyway, Mom, I think you should include this one and definitely this, it's really good. But for now, do you think we could clear the table and have supper? I'm starving."

After dinner they played Scrabble and Barbara almost beat her mom. It wasn't until she was in bed that she realized she had forgotten to ask for Dad's phone number in Toronto. Plenty of time, she thought sleepily. I'll pin her down tomorrow.

When Stan looked at the pictures next day he shook his head. "They all look so ordinary. I d-don't mean they're not good photographs, Mrs. Coutts. They're great. But I just can't think why you'd want to take them. This guy, for instance. Look at his face. You could pass it in a crowd a thousand times and never notice it. He could be the cornerstore owner."

"Let me see, Stan." Barb's mother looked over his shoulder. "Oh, *him*. He rather proves my point. This insignificant man knifed his mother and his mother's boyfriend, right here in Edmonton. As I said to Barbara, you really can't tell by appearances."

She began to pick up the pictures and arrange them in order. Stan was still holding the portrait of the murderer. He turned it over. "Jack Norton," he read aloud. "I remember reading about him. Lived not too far from here. It sounded like just an ordinary suburban family."

"Interested? You can keep it if you want. I've got a clearer one for the article."

"Thanks, Mrs. Coutts. I'd like to make a sketch from the photo. Are you coming out, Barb? We could take a sandwich."

"A bit cold for picnics, isn't it?" Mom put in.

"We know a cosy place out of the wind," said Barbara guardedly. "But I won't come now, Stan. I want to talk to Mom about something special, and she's a hard person to catch."

"That sounds serious," said her mother after Stan had gone. "I'll put the kettle on. Nothing wrong at school, is there? What about the gym trials? Everything all right there?"

"Yeah, everything's great. Mrs. Rawlings is driving us down to Calgary on Thursday afternoon. We'll be billeted with families there. After the trials are done on Friday we'll have a celebration dinner — well, I hope it'll be a celebration — and then we'll be driven back. We'll be home late, about eleven, I guess."

"This Thursday? How come I didn't know about it?"

"*Mom*, you signed a note!"

"I did? Yes, of course I did. I just needed reminding, that's all. Well, if it's not school or the trials, what's the problem?"

"You know my birthday's on Saturday?"

"I should. After all, I was *there*. Thirteen years ago. My goodness, it seems like yesterday — "

"Yes, Mom," she cut in ruthlessly. "So I was thinking . . ."

Why was it so difficult to talk about Dad? Because Mom had put up warning signs that said Keep Out, and No Questions, and now it was so long since Dad's name had been mentioned, that was why. It was her fault too. Since she had discovered Campbell's Bush she'd been too busy and involved to think much about Dad. But now her thirteenth birthday was only six days away and it was becoming urgent. She went at it in a rush, not even trying to be tactful.

"Do you have Dad's phone number in Toronto? I want to ask him to please come home for my birthday."

The laugh lines faded from Mom's face and it got tight and masklike, the way it had been right after Dad left. "I'm very sorry, Barb, but I don't have either your father's address or phone number. All communication between us has been through our lawyers."

"Then they could tell me. Can I ask them?"

Her mother shook her head. "It's not their business to tell us and they won't. Honey, if your father *does* remember your birthday you can be sure he'll be in touch with you. If not, well, would you really want a celebration based on your having to *remind* him?"

"I . . . I guess not. He *will* remember, though. I know he will."

Her mother didn't say anything. She poured another cup of tea and sat cradling the cup in her hands as if she were cold. Barbara went into the kitchen to make sandwiches for lunch and nothing more was said.

The gymnasts were excused school on Thursday. "Get as much sleep as you can," Mrs. Rawlings had counselled them the day before, but Barbara woke early and couldn't get back to sleep. She lay cosily under the covers, watching the light grow outside her window. Her overnight bag was already packed and ready by the front door.

After a time she couldn't bear lying still and jumped out of bed. She had a long shower and washed her hair. She was finishing a leisurely breakfast, while her mother typed at the other end of the table, when the phone rang.

"I'll get it." She licked marmalade off her fingers. "It's probably Alison or Jessica, wondering what to wear . . . Hullo? . . . Dad! Is it really you?" She clung to the phone as if it were a living link between her hand in Edmonton and Dad's in Toronto.

"Hi, chick, how've you been keeping? Is everything all right?" The light, amused voice hadn't changed at all.

"Everything's great, especially now you've phoned. You phoning was the only thing I wanted in the whole world. I just knew you'd — "

"As if I'd forget my only daughter's thirteenth birthday. How does it feel to be in your teens at last?"

"I don't know. I guess I won't know till Saturday. Dad, why didn't you write? It's been months and months."

"Sorry, chick. I've been run off my feet. I know you'll understand. The new business and well, everything."

"Y-yes. Anyway, it's great talking to you now. I've got something super special to ask you. Dad, could you possibly come to Edmonton this weekend? Please?"

His familiar laugh was as close as if he were in the same room. "You must be psychic, chick. I was planning to surprise you, but then I got cold feet and thought I'd better check. Do you mind it not being a surprise?"

Barbara felt happiness fizzing up inside her like a soft drink on a hot day. "You mean you *can* come? Oh, Dad . . ."

"I'm getting the afternoon plane for Edmonton today. There's some unfinished business that needs my attention this evening, and I've arranged to see a man first thing in the morning. After that I'm all yours. The whole of tomorrow. Get your mother to let you skip school — after all, it's only once — and I'll take you out to lunch, help you pick out a birthday present, tea somewhere nice, and then my plane back. What do you say?"

"But tomorrow's Friday!"

"I know that, chick. That's when I have an appointment to see this man. How about it? Aren't you thrilled?"

"Dad, I can't! We're leaving for Calgary this afternoon and we won't be back till really late tomorrow night."

"We?" The voice sounded cold and offended, not a bit like Dad.

"The school gym team. I haven't had a chance to tell you, because I couldn't write. I didn't have your address. I've been taking special gym classes and I've made it to the trials. Isn't it amazing? In my first term, at a new school and all! So you see we *have* to be in Calgary tomorrow, to try out for the Alberta junior team."

"Gym? That's not so important, is it?"

"Important? Dad, it's crucial! Mrs. Rawlings says that it's the first step to the Canadian games when we're a bit better, and then the Commonwealth Games."

"You don't really imagine that you're in that class, do you, chick?" He was laughing.

"I . . . I guess not. But I don't know till I try, do I? And I *am* good enough for the trials, Mrs. Rawlings says."

"So what this strange woman says is more important to you than a day with your dad?"

"No, of *course* not, Dad. And I'm free all Saturday and Sunday. Why can't we go out then? If I do well in Calgary it could be a double celebration."

"I'm sorry Barbara. I have to be back in Toronto tomorrow evening. I've promised Kristina that I'd help her put up the yacht for the winter. It's a lot of work and . . ."

Kristina? she thought. *Her.* And a yacht? His voice went on and on, driving her into a corner.

"So I guess you're going to have to choose between your father and this Mrs. Whatever-her-name-is."

"Dad, how *can* I choose? Hold on, just for a sec." Barbara turned to her mother, who was stacking the breakfast dishes with the blank expression of someone trying not to listen or get involved. "Mom, what *am* I to do? Tomorrow is the only day Dad can be here. But the trials . . . I've worked so hard. And I'd be letting down the others. And Mrs. Rawlings . . ."

"I can't tell you what to do, love. You'll have to make up your own mind and live with the consequences. That's part of growing up too." Her mother took the dishes into the kitchen.

Barbara put the phone to her ear. "Dad, are you still there?"

"Of course I'm here. I hope you've made up your mind. Don't listen to your mother, she'll just put you off. You decide for yourself."

"She hasn't. She wouldn't. She told me to make up my own mind."

"And?"

Barbara took a deep breath. "I choose to spend the day with you, Dad," she said quickly, in case her better self made her change her mind.

She was rewarded by her father's familiar chuckle in her ear. "There's my girl. Listen, chick. I'll rent a car at the airport when I get in this afternoon, and I'll get as much work done this evening as I can. That man I have to see tomorrow, I'll make it a breakfast meeting. I should be through before nine-thirty. The stores don't even open till ten, so we'll have lots of time together. If I get held up I'll phone you. Okay?"

"I'll be ready and waiting at nine-thirty. Dad, it's so great hearing from you again, I just can't believe it!"

"You too, chick." The line went dead.

Dad is coming. Dad is coming. She should be jumping up and down with happiness. Instead there was a sad, heavy feeling inside her chest. She went slowly into the kitchen. Mom was standing by the sink, looking out the window. Barb went up and stood behind her. There was nothing interesting out there. Only garbage cans.

"Mom, I decided to —"

"Go to Calgary!" Mom spun round, her face glowing.

"N-no. To . . . to lunch with Dad."

It was awful seeing the light fade out of Mom's face. Barbara suddenly wished that she could have the last five minutes over again, so that this time she could make the right decision. Would I have, though? she wondered. Or would I pick Dad over the team every time?

Mom smiled stiffly as if her face muscles hurt. "All right, dear. It's your decision. Now put your overnight bag back in your room and get ready for school. If you hurry you won't miss more than your first class."

"But why do I have to go? That's not fair, Mom."

"You were excused school only because of the Calgary trip. I'll give you a note for Mrs. Duvall excusing you from school tomorrow. And you must go to Mrs. Rawlings at once and explain why you're not going."

"Tell Mrs. Rawlings? Mom, I'd just die. Won't you phone her and explain? *Please*, Mom."

Her mother shook her head. "Certainly not. Barbara, *you* made the decision to skip the Calgary trials, and you're going to have to take the consequences."

"You just hate me, that's all," Barbara yelled. "Mothers are supposed to *help*. You're a rotten mother." She bolted upstairs to get ready for school. Now, added to the heavy lump in her chest was the terror of facing Mrs. Rawlings.

It was far worse than Barbara had imagined. Mrs. Rawlings' bony face went first white and then red at the news. "Just like that? Not going?"

"It's special, you see. My father's going to be in town. I haven't seen him since —"

"Spare me your whining, Barbara. Very well. Go join

your class. You're off the team, of course. That goes without saying."

"But, Mrs. Rawlings . . ."

"I haven't time for people who don't understand the meaning of the word *commitment*. Off you go now."

Barbara sat in a cubicle in the girls' washroom and cried. When she was through she washed her face in cold water and went into class. She sat with her head down, not saying a word or putting up her hand for the rest of the morning.

"What happened?" Stan asked at lunch time. "I thought you were off to Calgary."

"I don't want to talk about it."

"Okay. Don't get in a snit. Will you be going to you-know-where after school?"

"I don't know. Why don't you just go away and leave me alone?"

"Sure, I'll be glad to. Sorry for living. And I'll stay away from Campbell's Bush too. I wouldn't want to get in your highness's hair." He picked up his sandwiches and stalked off to the other end of the lunchroom.

Barbara bit her lip. She had never meant to quarrel with Stan. She wanted to run after him. *I didn't mean . . . I'm sorry* . . . But the words choked up in her throat and her legs wouldn't move.

The afternoon dragged by. At two-thirty she saw Alison and Jessica and the two girls from Grades Eight and Nine standing outside the school with their overnight bags. They were laughing and jigging excitedly from foot to foot. She should be with them. She should. She wanted to throw down her pencil and rush outside, yelling "Wait for me! It's a mistake! I've changed my mind!"

Mrs. Rawlings' station wagon pulled up and the four

scrambled in. It drove off. Barbara's pencil snapped in two and she looked down at her hands in surprise. They were trembling. She doubled them into fists and hid them under her desk so that no one would see.

"Barbara? Barbara, will you stop dreaming and pay attention! I've called on you twice already."

She spent the whole evening going through her clothes, trying to decide what to wear next day. But it was a lonely job. She couldn't phone Alison or Jessica and she certainly couldn't ask Mom's advice. In the end she pushed the whole mess onto the floor and went to bed, to lie staring at the ceiling, wondering how they were all getting on in Calgary.

Then she found herself thinking about Alison's cousin, Marianne, whose father had kidnapped her because he wanted her to live with *him*. Her heart beat rapidly as she wondered what she would do if Dad tried to kidnap *her*. She rolled over in bed, but her heart thumped even more loudly and she couldn't sleep. She rolled back again and looked at the grey square patch of window, and the glow from the fluorescent sign of Smith's Tool and Die Works.

What was she going to do if the developers arrived one morning soon and bulldozed the industrial park? I need my secret garden so much, she thought. She looked back to the first miserable days of her life in Westwood Acres and then to the discovery, the making of the reflecting pool and the bird table, the sharing of her secret with Stan. Building the little house together. Now it was all going to be destroyed. Maybe. And she'd ruined her friendship with Stan for no good reason. Maybe. She pounded her hot pillow and promised that she would try to make things all right with Stan, just as soon as Dad's visit was over.

She fell asleep into a muddled dream. She was standing in front of the fence that hid Campbell's Bush. A bulldozer was lumbering down the passage towards her. She yelled, "Stan, help!" and, in the instant before the bulldozer ran her down, she saw the driver's face — and it was Stan's.

Then her alarm shrilled in her ears. She'd set it extra early so she'd have time to wash and dry her hair. By nine-thirty she was sitting tidily in the living room in her dark red and grey pleated skirt with the matching red angora sweater. The skirt was almost too short, she'd grown so much this year, but it was by far the nicest thing she had. Her nails were clean and her hair shone. She sat at the window so she could see the car pull up.

"The time'll pass more quickly if you do something, Barb."

"Like what?"

"You could pick up your room."

"*Mom*. For crying out loud! I don't want to get messed up."

"You could read a book."

"I couldn't keep my mind on it. He'll be here in a minute. It's only a quarter to ten."

"Honey, don't count on —"

"You're just being mean, Mom. He *promised*. He'll be here or he'll phone."

Her mother opened her mouth and shut it again. Barbara went on looking out the window. Ten o'clock. She stood up and shook the pleats in her skirt straight and sat down again. Ten-thirty . . .

"Would you like a glass of milk and a cookie, love?"

"Don't fuss, Mom. I'm fine."

At eleven the phone rang and she leapt for it. A woman's voice asked for Miss Coutts.

"That's me."

"Your father asked me to let you know that he was going to be a little late, Miss Coutts." Click. Dial tone.

"Thank you," she said into the dead phone. She went slowly upstairs and picked up all the clothes she had thrown on the floor last night. When that was done she put her used socks and panties in the hamper. She sorted her tapes and tidied the books on her shelves. Her room looked strangely cold and unlived in when she was done.

She leaned her elbows on the window sill and looked across the road at Smith's Tool and Die Works. She tried very hard *not* to think about Alison and Jessica. Would they be working on the uneven bars by now? Or the rings? Jessica's weak spot was her wrists, though her balance and timing were great.

The doorbell! She leaned out the window and saw a strange car at the curb. She closed her window and walked slowly downstairs. It was a quarter to one. She picked up her purse.

"I'll see you later, Mom."

Mom came into the hall to kiss her goodbye, but Barb waved and went out quickly so Mom wouldn't see her face.

"Sorry to be a bit late." Dad pushed the near door open for her to get in, so she didn't even have a chance to hug him. She'd been looking forward to that hug. She fastened her seat belt.

He drove fast, the way he always did. She glanced at him shyly. He was different somehow, something about his clothes or the way he wore them. Nothing she could exactly put her finger on, but it was a bit like going out with a stranger.

Lunch was better. Dad had picked a fancy restaurant and, though there was a little fuss at first over their arriving an hour after the time of their reservation, everything was soon arranged comfortably. She saw Dad pass a folded bill to the man who showed them to their table.

He made silly jokes over the names of the dishes on the menu and then helped her pick out her favourite things. For a while she was able to joke back, but then it was hard to find anything to talk about. School took only a couple of sentences, and she could see he wasn't really interested. She couldn't bear to talk about gym and had to steer clear of Campbell's Bush and therefore of Stan. This didn't leave much. She sipped a Shirley Temple while Dad got through a couple of scotches and ordered a third.

"So tell me about *your* life," she said brightly, when the silence had gone on too long. "Describe where you live, so I can imagine you being there."

"Actually it's pretty marvellous, chick. It's a condo down at Harbourfront. Just imagine what it's like living in a major city, a place where all the action is, and still having the whole of Lake Ontario at your doorstep and a yacht moored down below."

"A yacht sounds awfully grand, Dad. You must be doing really well to be able to buy a yacht." Just for a minute Barbara thought, with a twinge, of the hours Mom spent at the typewriter and the stacks of boring peanut butter sandwiches they had eaten.

Dad fingered his tie in an unfamiliar gesture. "Actually,

the yacht belongs to Kristina. The condo was hers too, though of course I'm sharing the expenses now."

Mom would never have picked out that tie, Barbara thought, and began to realize that indeed it must be this Kristina person who was choosing all Dad's suits and shirts and ties, who presumably cooked his breakfasts and who took him sailing in her yacht. She put a piece of butter-tender filet mignon in her mouth and began to chew. It felt like cardboard.

Dad was still talking and she dragged her attention back from her private thoughts. "And we really must arrange for you to come and stay with us sometime. You'll love Toronto. There's so much going on."

"Could I go sailing with you, do you suppose? I mean you and me, by ourselves?"

"I don't know about that, chicken. You're a big girl now, so I know you'll understand. Since the yacht is Kristina's I can hardly take you out in it without her. She might get upset. Anyway, she's a much better sailor than I am. Safer to have her along."

Safer. That was never one of Dad's words.

They ordered dessert: croquembouche, tiny spheres of fluffy pastry with cream in the middle and spun sugar all over the outside, taken off a great tower of them. It was awe-inspiring, and for a moment Barbara devoted herself to eating something she wouldn't be getting for a very long time.

After her curiosity was satisfied she asked again. "When can I come, Dad? Soon?"

"Maybe we could arrange for you to come east for part of next summer's holidays. How about that? By then I should be able to take some time off and show you around."

"Next *summer*? Dad, won't I even get to see you at *Christmas*?"

"It's a bit complicated, chick. I've got to get Kristina used to the idea that I've got a daughter who's practically grown up. And very beautiful too." He laughed in a way that set her teeth on edge.

I hate what you're doing and what you're turning into. You're not like the Dad I remember at all, she wanted to shout across the white tablecloth and the remains of their dessert. I'm not beautiful and you know it. I'm skinny and my braces won't be out for another year. I loved you and I thought you loved me too. But you don't. You only care about yourself and maybe this Kristina person.

She forced herself to lay her fork neatly at the edge of her plate and fold her hands in her lap as if nothing was wrong. Dad looked at his watch and signalled the waiter.

As he signed the credit slip he said, quite casually, "Look, it's nearly three-thirty, later than I thought. My plane leaves at five-thirty and it'll take an hour in that traffic to get to the airport. No time for decent shopping and there's no fun in rushing it, is there? Why don't I just drive you home the long way round?"

The pain inside Barbara was like the yolk of an egg, still in its fragile shell. If she moved carefully and didn't say anything out of the ordinary or emotional, she should be able to get home without it breaking. Though how can I face Mom? she thought. I'll never be able to fool Mom, not for an instant.

"I think that's a good idea," she found herself saying. "It's awful having to rush, and the airport security might hold you up."

"There's my girl." At last he gave her the hug she'd

been wanting so badly. Only now it didn't mean anything at all. She had to hold herself back or the shell
might break and all the pain come pouring out right
in the middle of the restaurant among the plush seats
and white tablecloths and chandeliers. He would be so
embarrassed.

Dad still drove too quickly, although there was lots of
time. He cut in front of slower drivers and took risky left
turns, but she didn't feel frightened this time. Just numb.
Even though he'd said he'd drive the long way round,
which meant through the river valley, it seemed no time
before they had pulled up in front of the house. Dad took
out his wallet, folded a bill and tucked it into her
hand.

"For tomorrow, birthday girl. With my love."

"Thank you, Dad. And for my lovely lunch too." Her
cheeks felt stiff and she had to force her lips to form the
correct words, as if she were manipulating a puppet.
"Have a safe trip back," she managed to say. She
scrambled out of the car, slammed the door and ran up the
path to the house, fumbling for her door key.

"Why, Barb, you're home early!"

"Yes. Dad had to catch the five-thirty plane. We only
had time for lunch. Nothing else."

"Honey, I'm so sorry."

Barbara looked at her mother. She'd grown a lot this
summer and fall. She was almost as tall as Mom and could
look straight into her eyes. In them she saw Mom's pain
and the truth that Mom had known all along, that Dad
wasn't to be trusted, that he made promises and didn't
keep them, that he hadn't quite grown up yet and would
only look after himself, making sure that *he* was
comfortable.

What a I fool I've been, she thought bitterly. I've been filling myself up with dreams of a father who didn't even exist.

"Barbara, are you all right?"

"Sure. It was a fantastic lunch. Just out of this world." She forced the tears back. "Here, Mom. Dad gave me this. I don't need a thing and I know you're short a lot of the time. Use it for groceries or something." As she pushed the money into Mom's hand she noticed that it was a hundred-dollar bill.

"But . . . my dear . . ."

She could feel her face breaking into little pieces like a mud mask. "And . . . and I'm sorry I've been so rotten to you. I'm going for a walk. I don't think I'll be able to manage any supper for ages."

She walked blindly down the road, still clutching her purse, seeing herself in a new and unflattering light. Why, I'm like *him*. I've been so selfish and mean to Mom. I just wish I could have this whole summer and fall to live over again, I'd do it better, I swear. I wish miracles happened. I wish we could be back to where we were when we moved to Westwood, Mom and me. I'd keep my room tidy and help out in the house more. Maybe I could get a part-time job and give her all my earnings. But that's stupid. She'd never let me do that. My marks aren't high enough. All she wants is for me to do well at school and keep out of trouble. Boring old school. Maybe I *could* try. Would she know it was because I was sorry and I do love her, if I got higher marks?

Dad, you'll be halfway to the airport now in your flashy rented car. And you don't know how I feel and you don't care. But maybe I'm wrong. Maybe deep inside you do. But I don't understand grownups, and I wish I didn't have to become one, because I don't think I like them very much. Except for Mom. Mom's okay.

She looked up. How dark it was getting! The western sky was barred with black clouds that hid the setting sun. She looked around. She was standing in the middle of 113th Avenue, close to the secret passage, though she hadn't even been aware that that was where her feet had carried her.

Well, where else could she go to be alone? Campbell's Bush was her refuge. There was nowhere else *to* go. She wiped the tears from her face with her woolly glove and turned into the passage.

It was even darker in here. *Go home*, a voice said inside her. Not yet, she answered. I don't want Mom to see me in this mess, not till I've got myself straightened out.

Slowly, almost reluctantly, she climbed the fence. The garden was a deep pool of darkness, but at the eastern end the orange glow of the Coleman stove seemed to greet her. So Stan was here after all. I'm so glad I didn't put him off yesterday, she thought. Though I was awfully mean. Suppose he won't speak to me?

But Stan wouldn't be like that, she realized with a sudden spark of gladness in the dark of her misery. Stan was the same clear through. If he was here, it was because he'd understand that it hadn't been Barbara yelling at him yesterday but her unhappiness. Stan would understand. And Stan would help her. With a huge wet sniff she dropped down into the shadowy safety of the secret garden.

NINE

Barbara scrubbed her eyes with the back of her hand and walked carefully along the narrow path they had worn down along the northern wall and across to the lean-to. Everything looked blurry through her tears. I hope my face isn't *too* awful, she thought, and she made her voice sound extra bright, as though nothing was wrong.

"Stan, I'm so glad you decided to come after all. I'm sorry I was so rude to you yesterday. Please forget it and talk to me."

Stan's back was towards her, the pattern of the eagle on his Cowichan sweater stretched across his shoulders. He didn't turn or say a word.

"Please, Stan. I've made such an idiot of myself and I'm so miserable." She suppressed a sob and turned it into an awkward laugh. "What's the matter, Stan? I know I was a bit of a stinker, but I wasn't that bad, was I? For goodness sake. . . !"

As she squatted in her usual place by the camp stove

the shadowy figure — it seemed to have been frozen, it was so still — turned towards her. At first her brain refused to believe what her eyes clearly told it in spite of the gathering shadows and her tears. Then she let out a gasp that was almost a groan. Because it wasn't Stan! It was a total stranger, wearing Stan's old sweater and sitting in Stan's place, stirring soup in a pan on Stan's stove.

It was like the terror of nightmare, in which the familiar suddenly becomes terrifying. And, as in nightmare, Barbara felt time slow down, stop, wait between two ticks of a clock as she went on staring at the unfamiliar face, her mouth open, her lips drying.

This man's hair was cut short, army-style, and his face was smooth and unlined, the forehead running back to a slightly receding hairline. His nose had no particular shape, and his eyes were wary but otherwise unremarkable. He could have been any age from thirty to forty. He was a total stranger, yet Barb had an odd feeling she knew him.

The man's lips moved and time began to run normally again.

"What the hell are you doing in my place?" His hand shot out and grabbed her wrist just as she scrambled to her feet. She tried to pull away, but his grip was powerful.

"Let me go ! It's not yours anyway. It's mine. I found it and Stan and I built the lean-to, and the purple martins' house and the pond — "

"Pond! Stupid idea that. I was going to light a fire, the way I used to, down in the middle there, and I fell in your fool pond. Soaked my boots and socks. Then I saw this little hut and the stove. Good idea, the stove, no one can't see the smoke from that."

"You were never here before. You're making it up.

There was grass knee-high everywhere, no sign of a fire."

He laughed bitterly. "I'm talking about fifteen years ago, kid. That's when I discovered Jack's Castle."

"Jack's . . .?"

"This place. I'm Jack, see. It was a kind of fancy of mine, naming it."

"*We* call it Campbell's Bush."

"Please yourself. But it was Jack's Castle first. Don't you forget it. You shouldn't have come. It's my place and I need it. I had it in mind all the time I was inside . . . funny, that, because I hadn't thought of it in years, not in years. Then it all came back to me, so when I gave them the slip I made straight for it, never even sure it'd still be here. They've built all over it by now, I told myself. You can't go back, not ever. But there it was, only the little trees fifteen years taller. Like a miracle. Then I saw the shelter, all the comforts of home. Stove, sweater, soup and canned stuff. Wish you'd left some cigarettes, though. Got any with you?"

"Course not. Smoking's stupid. It shortens your life."

He laughed till he choked, till there were tears in his eyes. Barbara pulled away, but his grip on her wrist tightened.

"What's wrong? Are you all right?"

"Yeah, I'm all right. Why shouldn't I be all right? Are you kids lovers? This your secret place?"

"Lovers? Goodness, no." She felt her face getting hot. "We're only in Grade Seven. I'm thirteen. Almost. Tomorrow." Her voice wobbled.

"Geez! *Thirteen?* You didn't ought to have come."

"I'm sorry. I didn't mean to intrude. If you just let go

my wrist I'll go away and leave you in peace. You're right — Jack's Castle was here before Campbell's Bush." She got slowly to her knees, pulling gently at her arm.

"Don't do that. You can't leave. You know that."

"But I *must*. I told my mother I was just going for a walk. It'll be suppertime and there'll be an awful fuss."

"A walk, you told her?" He pounced like a cat on a bird. "You didn't tell her you were coming here, did you? She doesn't know about it, does she? No, of course not. That's the whole point of this place, isn't it? That the grownups don't know about it."

"But of *course* Mom knows," Barbara lied valiantly. "I tell her everything. If I'm not home soon she'll have the police here in no time."

The hand on her wrist tightened until she gasped. "Don't lie. I hate liars. They make me —" The pressure increased and Barbara's knees collapsed and she fell back into a crouch, tears of pain springing into her eyes. Mercifully the hand released her, and she sat up and massaged her aching wrist.

"That's better. Stay still, little girl, and don't do anything stupid. I don't want you bugging me, okay? I got to think."

Barbara told herself that if she were calm and ordinary then maybe he'd stop being hyper and let her go. She could promise never to come back, not to tell on him. When the moment was right she could persuade him, couldn't she? She battened down the fear that kept surging up, making her want to scream and scream. She would be calm and she would be allowed to go. She wouldn't let her mind think of any possible alternatives.

In the silence the soup hissed against the sides of the pan.

"Excuse me, Jack."

"Don't bug me, I said, didn't I?"

"But the pan's going to boil over. Let me . . ." She reached towards the stove. Into her mind flashed the possibility of throwing the hot soup into his face and making a dash for it.

But he pushed her hand aside. "Keep off." He grabbed the handle, let out a yell and dropped the pan on the ground. "Oh, geez, oh hell . . ." He bent over, his scalded hand tucked into his armpit, and swore viciously without stopping for what felt to Barbara like five minutes. She crouched, her hands over her ears, until the monotonous voice stopped.

Silence. She could hear her heart thump. The wind rustled the dry grass.

"It didn't get spilled. Here, have a cup." The voice was apologetic. He poured the soup into the two mugs as if nothing had happened.

She sat up and took the proffered cup, cradling it between icy hands, inhaling the salty steam.

"I didn't ought to have talked like that. Guess you're not used to that kind of language."

She shook her head.

"Nice cosy middle-class family, I bet. Lots to eat and a nice mommy and daddy."

"More or less," she managed to say. "They're divorced though. My Dad lives in Toronto."

"That's a dirty shame. Families ought to stick together. Was that why you were blubbing when you come in? Geez, you scared the hell out of me. I thought . . ." He stopped.

Barbara took a sip of her chicken noodle soup. Its salty warmth crept through her body, giving her a kind of artificial courage. You can talk people out of things, she told herself. Like people in hijacked airplanes did. It worked. Sometimes it worked.

"Dad left home in May," she said into the silence of the garden. "He went off to Toronto with a young woman he met at a New Year's party and left Mom to manage."

"You been hungry since?"

"Certainly not! We've had a lot of boring macaroni cheese dinners and peanut butter sandwiches, but Mom's done all right. She's a writer. She works really hard. We moved to a rental townhouse. It's okay, I guess. Then I discovered Campbell's Bush — I'm sorry, I mean — "

"That's okay. You call it your name and I'll call it mine. Just so you remember who found it first. Go on."

"I kept expecting to hear from Dad. After all, he'd been married to Mom for fifteen years. He'd known *me* for thirteen. I couldn't believe that he'd go away and not even *write*. Then I hoped he'd come for my thirteenth birthday and he did. But he made me choose . . . to go out with him or go to Calgary with the team for the gym trials."

"And you made the wrong choice?"

Barbara nodded. The tears were running down her face, but it didn't seem to matter. "He was so rotten, Jack. He was four hours late, so there was only time for lunch. Then he tried to make it up to me by giving me a hundred dollars, instead of us going out to choose a birthday present together. So I knew he didn't care."

"A hundred dollars? You got it with you, kid? Here." He grabbed her purse and turned it upside down, scattering comb and lipstick, tissue and coins and bus tickets.

"I gave it to Mom for groceries, as soon as I got home. I didn't want to touch it."

"A hundred bucks would have been real handy right now."

"I'm sorry," said Barbara sadly. "You'd have been welcome to it."

"I'll manage without. It'd have made things easier, that's all. Let that be a lesson to you, kid. Don't trust people. They'll always let you down. You were stupid, weren't you? He'd left you and your mom and didn't even write. So why'd you trust him?"

"Because he's my dad, I guess. Maybe he was selfish. And maybe he *did* let me down. But you're wrong about not trusting people. You have to."

"Then what the hell are you going on like a watering can for?"

Barbara sniffed. "Don't you see? I'm crying for *me*. I let down the team and ruined my chances with them, just because I got suckered into thinking that a day with Dad was worth letting down my friends and losing my . . . my . . ."

"Your what?"

"Respect, I guess. The respect of my friends at school. My respect for *me*. You know what I mean?"

"No. It sounds like a proper load of garbage. Respect for yourself? The only time you can respect yourself is when you're two steps ahead of the next guy."

Barbara shook her head. "You're wrong. Dad thinks like that too, and he's miserable inside. I could tell, all the time we were supposed to be having a great time at lunch." She blew her nose. "Why do you think it'll work your way?"

"Because that's the way the world is. You're not out of the egg yet, are you? Just a child."

"Being a child doesn't mean being stupid. Maybe

you've forgotten. Fifteen years ago, wasn't it?"

"What was?"

"Jack's Castle. I bet you were different then. When you found it."

"I was fourteen then. Not much older than you. About a hundred years older in some things, though, I'll bet. Falling into Jack's Castle was like magic. All that stuff about wishes and dragons and unicorns, that's what it was like. I'd been into the stores when they were closed, see, just having a look around. This radio shop had a fancy new alarm system I hadn't been expecting. I heard the cops coming and I nipped up on the roof of a warehouse on 111th Avenue to get away from them. So there I was, on the roofs, dodging along, it's amazing how they connect together, almost like roadways. And then I saw it. Little trees and grass and stuff. As secret as secret. Without thinking I just dropped off the roof into the grass. I remember it smelled sweet, like honey. And the sky was a big blue square, peaceful, with no cops interfering."

"Had the fence been put up then?"

"Yeah." He laughed. "I'd been lying there for a bit, getting my breath back, enjoying the peace and quiet, and I suddenly thought — Geez! Suppose all the walls are joined together, there's no way out except straight up, which I'm not likely to make, not being a fly. I'll starve to death, I thought, and no one the wiser. So I scrambled to my feet, my heart banging away inside me, and there was the fence. I hopped over and down the passage. The tracks were brighter then and there weren't all them weeds. I nearly missed it this time, it's got so overgrown."

"Did you go back to Jack's Castle again, after that day?"

"All the time. Whenever I needed to get away from my mother interfering, or the police or any of that lot. I was safe in Jack's Castle. I could count on it. It was better than home, except I didn't have no fancy lean-to or stove or nothing like you've got."

"I wouldn't either, if Stan hadn't helped me."

"I remember there was a bit of a gap at one end of the fence and once I saw animal tracks, so I set string snares along by it. Caught a big jackrabbit too. Dunno who was the most surprised, him or me. I broke his neck and skinned him and cooked the meat over a campfire, down in the middle where you've got that stupid pond. Bit tough, but not bad. I saved the skin, but I didn't know how to cure it, so the maggots got in. In the end I buried it. Under the big maple over there. Not that it was big then. Scrawny little sapling, the way I was then. That's where I carved my initials."

"On the maple? I never saw. If I'd seen them I'd have known that I wasn't really the first person here. I'm glad I didn't know. It always made me feel special, coming here, like Columbus or Darien or Neil Armstrong."

"I don't know about that Columbus Darien stuff. To me this place was always: 'I'm King of the Castle. Get off, you dirty rascal.' Which is why I called it Jack's Castle on account of it was mine and no one else's and nobody'd got no right to push me around or nothing while I was here. It was a good feeling."

"D'you know what I just thought, Jack? Maybe there was a kid fifteen years before you . . . if the secret garden was here thirty years ago."

"It might have been. Yeah, I like that. Some poor little guy with a dad what left him and a mom what lied. Maybe there *was* someone like that. Maybe they put their initials on the maple too."

Jack chuckled, and the fear that had been mounting inside Barbara subsided a little. His anger and his wild laughter were two equally terrifying extremes. Somewhere in the middle, between the two, there might still be a person she could talk to and even reason with.

In a strange way, she found she was becoming involved, not with the terrifying smooth-faced stranger, but with the boy he had been fifteen years ago. Only fifteen years? She would have guessed that he was well over thirty. Twenty-nine? What had happened to him in those years to make him look middle-aged? Could she get back to the fourteen-year-old boy inside this angry man?

"Let's go see." He got up and pulled her to her feet.

"What? Go where?" Her heart leapt. Maybe he was going to take her out of Campbell's Bush. Once outside the trap of the garden she could run for it. She could scream . . .

"Let's go see where I carved my initials. See if anyone else done it earlier."

"Will we be able to see anything?" Barbara looked around, startled to see just how dark it had grown while they talked. The sun had just set and the lemon-yellow western sky was barred with black clouds.

"Don't you have a flashlight in that fancy cooler?"

"Never thought of it. We're never here after dark."

"It's all right. There's enough light." He dragged her across the plot of grass.

"Watch out for the pond," she said, just in time.

"You didn't ought to put things like that in my place."

"I'm sorry, Jack. I didn't know."

"That's all right." His voice was a kid's, sulky but okay. He strode across to the larger of the two maples and peered at its trunk. "I carved it at shoulder-level, just about here. Can't you see?"

"I can't see a thing, honestly, Jack."

"You must. It's got to be here. I couldn't have dreamed anything as real as that, could I? I remembered Jack's Castle and it was right here. I came to it direct, fifteen years later. So I couldn't have dreamt I carved my initials, could I?" His voice rose.

Barbara peered frantically at the maple's grey trunk. It really was very dark. In the square of garden, twilight settled in like soft mud. She ran her hands over the bark. Fifteen years ago. Who had grown most since then, Jack or the tree? She reached up, above eye-level.

"Jack, you're a lot taller than me. Can you see where my fingers are . . . there's something."

"That's it, kid! I told you, didn't I? J.N. . . . Jack Norton. I *knew* I hadn't dreamed it. Now we've got to check if someone else put theirs on it before me."

His voice rose excitedly and he edged around the tree, his hands feeling the bark above his head. Barbara glanced furtively at the distance between her and the fence. Could she? No, she wouldn't stand a chance. He was much bigger than she was and much younger than she'd hoped.

"I can't feel nothing. What about you?"

"Not a sign. I guess that makes you the first for sure, Jack."

He chuckled again. "You know what I'm going to do, kid? I'm going to carve 'number one' under my initials so

114

anyone else coming in here will know that that's what I am. What d'you think of that?"

"I think it's a great idea. But what about light? Will you be able to see?"

"You should have a flashlight, you really should." She could feel the anger under the surface.

"There's matches," she said quickly. "You must have used them for the Coleman. There's a big box in the cooler, if you put them back. Hold on. I'll get them."

She ran back, thinking as she went: the *knife*. It was a solid kitchen knife she'd borrowed from Mom's kitchen. It dated back to the time when Mom had gone through a *haute cuisine* stage, buying copper pots and a whole set of Henckel's knives, sharp as razors and solidly made. Now that she and her mom were in a can-opener stage, she knew Mom wouldn't miss one, and she'd found it handy for slicing bread and canned lunch meat.

She threw back the lid of the cooler and scrabbled through it in the darkness. That odd shape must be the can-opener. She felt a couple of spoons. The tines of a fork jabbed her in the palm. Fat lot of use a *fork* would be as a weapon. *Where* was the knife?

"What's the matter with you? Hurry up. I want to do it *now*."

"Just a sec. It's so dark over here." Her hand closed around the box of matches. "Got them. I'm coming."

She picked her way back across the darkening garden to where Jack was standing, his hands moving lovingly over the initials he had carved fifteen years before.

"Come on, then. Strike a match so I can see what I'm doing."

It was the strangest thing that had ever happened to

Barbara. As the match flared up, the darkness was pushed away and for a moment she held a small sphere of light that showed her hands, the textured bark of the maple tree, his hands and the knife they held.

Her mother's kitchen knife. The one with the fifteen-centimetre blade, as sharp as a razor.

"Hold it steady. What's the matter with you?" he snarled as her hand shook.

"S-sorry." The light guttered and the darkness rushed in, blacker than ever. She struck another match and held it aloft. The blade winked wickedly in the flame as he gouged at the bark with its point. The light faded to a blue bead and he swore at her again.

"It does take two hands to strike a match." She tried to keep her voice matter-of-fact. She held up the third match, the flame quivering in her hand. She willed her hand not to shake, the flame to burn straight and clear. She stared at the heart of the flame and it steadied her.

After six matches Jack had gouged out "#1," and two matches later he had deepened the lines and smoothed them to his satisfaction.

"There. Now there'll be no arguments about who got here first."

"It looks really neat."

"I'd have done better with a proper penknife, but it's not bad. Now I'm going to do yours underneath."

"All right. Unless you'd like me to do it . . ."

"It's my knife," he snapped.

"All right, all right. No problem."

"What's your name, then?"

"Barbara Coutts."

"Okay. B.C. it is."

As she lit the matches and held them steady, one by one, and watched the tip of the knife gouge into the bark, Barbara felt panic rising inside her. Until now this man had been more of an abstract idea, a man who had been in prison, perhaps for stealing or forging cheques, something safe and ordinary like that. She had concentrated on that being the kind of person he was.

Now the initials and the name for which they stood, J.N. for Jack Norton, suddenly clicked in her mind. She could see his photograph as clearly as if she were standing at the dining table in her safe, normal home. J.N., Jack Norton, murderer, the man with the face that had interested Stan because it was so very ordinary.

Only two matches remained in the box. If the matches were gone before he finished he might lose his temper again. And he had the knife.

"B.C. #2. D'you like it? It's good, isn't it?" His look was eager and like a child's in the flicker of the last match.

"It's great. Thank you. I've never had my initials carved on a tree before. I never thought of doing it myself."

"That's just because girls aren't smart at things like that," he said confidently.

She bit her lip and forced a smile. "I expect you're right. Now you've finished would you like a cup of cocoa? Or I could cook up something if you're hungry."

"What else you got? I just grabbed the soup because it was easy."

"Let's look." She led the way back to the lean-to and hauled the cooler closer to the stove so that the glimmer of light from it let her read the labels. "I've got a can of lunch meat. No bread for sandwiches, I'm afraid, but it's nice sliced and fried."

"Okay. Go ahead."

She zipped off the lid with the key attached to the bottom and turned it out onto its lid. "I need the knife to slice it, Jack." She held her hand out casually.

He almost fell for it. She could see the automatic response in his arm. Then he stiffened. "You can't have it. It's mine."

"No, it's my mother's. I borrowed it and put it in the cooler. You found it there, remember?"

"Your mother's?" His mouth fell open and his face lost its boyish look and became older, the way it had been when she first saw him. "Your mother's knife? Oh, no. No. No." He shook his head over and over.

Barbara licked her dry lips and tried to smile. "Maybe I'm wrong. One knife is like another, isn't it? Here, you slice the meat while I heat the frying pan."

He calmed down and sliced the meat carefully for her. She fried the slices and added broken crackers to the juices. He ate it all out of the pan, gobbling the meat and spooning up the crackers with the fat.

It was very dark now. When she looked up at the square of sky above Campbell's Bush, she could see nothing. The sky was overcast. Would there be a moon later? She couldn't remember. Mom must be missing her. She'd be getting worried. What would she do? Call the police or wait? But even if she *did* call the police it wouldn't help. Mom didn't know about Campbell's Bush. She could be here for days and nobody would know.

If she could just distract Jack long enough to vault over the fence she could run across 113th Avenue and hide in the laneway to the north, maybe even inside one of the big industrial disposal bins. If she could just get a head start . . .

"That was good." He smacked his lips and wiped his

hand across his greasy mouth. "You know, you gave me quite a turn when you said my knife was your mom's."

"How come?" Barbara found herself asking and tried to bite back the words, too late. Oh, no, I don't want to know. I don't.

"It was *her* knife I did it with, see? When I caught her in the house with her fancy man and she hit me. It was just once too often, that's all. That's what I told them. She never did think I'd amount to anything. A weakling, she called me. A pansy, rotten things like that. She'd never have believed that I'd go downstairs and take the knife out of the kitchen drawer, right out of the drawer."

Barbara sat without breathing, her nails digging into the palms of her hands.

"It was as easy as killing the rabbit. Easier. The rabbit was kind of pretty. I wouldn't have killed *it* if I hadn't been hungry. I don't think I would have. And you know, when I'd done it to her and him too, I felt such a lightness, like a great rock I'd been carrying on my back all those years had rolled off."

"It's okay." The words came from her dry lips to fill the silence.

"I don't want to talk about it. I don't think about it anymore. It was just you talking about your mom's knife brought it back."

"That's okay. Don't think about it. You're safe in Jack's Castle." She managed to keep her voice steady, comforting, and she could sense his anger ease away. She was icy cold and it was hard not to shiver. If she began shivering she wouldn't be able to stop and he would get mad.

The light from the stove seemed to be fading. Was it

going to run out of fuel? Or was she going to faint? She had fainted once in assembly back at Willow Heights and it had felt like this. Cold and dark. What would he do if she did faint? Would he panic and kill her? She took a deep breath and stared across the blackness of Campbell's Bush. The far wall seemed a very long way off, as if she were looking at it through the wrong end of a telescope. She knew now she could never climb the fence. She no longer had the strength to escape, even if she had the opportunity. The fence that had protected and enclosed the secret garden had become the bars of a terrifying prison.

TEN

Terry was worried. He'd had to go for an eye examination and it had upset his whole routine. He had missed afternoon school and therefore wasn't able to shadow Stan to his secret place and keep guard. Eye doctors! He was sure none of the spies in the books he read went to an eye doctor.

He scurried through the streets towards the secret garden. The lights came on overhead, magically haloed because of the drops in his eyes. Late, I'm late. Letting Stan down, he thought. Suppose this is the one time someone else comes along, interfering? And I'm not there.

Out of breath and sweating, he plunged into the passage, looking over his shoulder as he did. There was always the fear that either Stan or Barbara would come along behind him and his secret vigil would become

121

public knowledge. But it was all right. No one was in sight.

He crept up to the fence and crouched to look through the crack. He could see them clearly enough in the glow of the Coleman stove in spite of his bleary eyes. Stan was in his familiar Cowichan sweater and he'd know Barbara anywhere by the long straight dark hair. They had something in their hands. Something hot.

Terry longed for a cup of something hot too. For a moment he thought longingly of the tea and crumpets cooling on the tray at home; then he put them firmly out of his mind and settled himself as comfortably as possible with his back against the west wall of the passage. After all, spies weren't supposed to be as comfortable as the people they were sworn to protect. He took a Mars bar from the pocket of his windbreaker and ate it slowly. He blinked his bleary eyes. Then something happened that had never happened to him before. He dozed off in the middle of his self-appointed vigil.

Stan walked home from school on Friday in a sour mood. He wanted to go to Campbell's Bush and draw in the little daylight that was left. But the secret garden was Barbara's by right of discovery, even if he had invested a lot of time and ingenuity in making it more comfortable. Since she'd made such a point of wanting to be left alone, then he'd stay away. He wouldn't go near the place until she said it was okay.

"Just go away and leave me alone," she'd snarled at him, as if they weren't friends, as if they hadn't shared important private thoughts. Wasn't that being a friend? Trusting each other? And yet she'd looked at him as if he were a stranger. The more he thought about the expression on her face the more wretched he felt.

He dumped his books in the hall and went into the kitchen for a snack. Josef was there ahead of him.

"Haven't seen your shining face around here for a while. What's the matter? Your best girl let you down?"

"Why don't you shut up?" Stan poured himself a glass of milk, grabbed a handful of cookies and went upstairs.

Friday evening. The whole of Saturday and Sunday stretched ahead of him like a desert with no oasis in sight. He got out his homework and stared at it. It was no good. He couldn't concentrate. Restlessly he wandered up and down his room, picked up the photograph that Mrs. Coutts had given him and studied it. It was such a boring face . . . yet there must be something hidden in it, some indication of the secret behind it. What made a man a murderer? Absently his hand reached for a pencil and he began to sketch the features. He was still working on it when Mom called him down for supper.

They were just finishing off Mom's raisin pie when the phone rang. Josef leapt for it.

"Hey, it's for you, kid brother. A Mrs. Coutts."

"*Mrs.* Coutts? You must have got it wrong." Stan uncurled his legs from under the table, trying to keep the pleased expression off his face. So Barbara was sorry she'd snapped at him. She wanted to make it up. He'd be able to spend his weekend at Campbell's Bush after all. He threw his boredom off like a pair of runners.

"Hi, Stan here."

But it *was* Mrs. Coutts. A Mrs. Coutts whose voice he

didn't recognize right away, a voice gone high and almost hysterical, beginning sentences and leaving them half-finished.

"Is Barbara over there, Stan?"

"Here? You mean at my house? No, Mrs. Coutts. Sh-should she be?"

"When she went off . . . she was in such a state . . . just a walk, she said . . . I didn't think, not then . . . but it's been *hours*."

"Well, I'm sorry, but she's not here. I haven't seen her all day. She wasn't in school."

"I know *that*. Her father . . . I should never have . . . but how was I to know? And how could I stop him?"

"Maybe she's still with him." It seemed so obvious. He scratched one calf with the sole of the other foot. Josef was looking irritated, wanting him to get off the phone.

"No, of course not. I mean, I wouldn't be worrying . . . well, I suppose I would, but in a different way. What I mean is he dropped her off at the house. She *can't* be with him . . . going for a walk, she said . . . she was in such a state . . ." Her voice trailed off. He thought he heard a sob at the other end of the phone. It made his brain start working.

"She was upset at school yesterday too, Mrs. Coutts. Look, I have an idea where she might be. I'll go see if I can find her."

"Just give me the address. I'll drive. Just tell me where."

Stan ran his hand through his hair. "It's not . . . not that sort of place. I mean, there isn't an address exactly. I could be wrong anyway. Look, I'll go right now and look for her. Then I'll come and tell you one way or the other. Okay?"

"Thank you, Stan. You're my only hope. Alison and Jessica, they're both in Calgary, so she can't be at their homes . . . you don't suppose she . . . ?"

"I'm sure there's nothing to worry about. I'll be off now, Mrs. Coutts. I'll see you soon."

Stan ran along the deserted avenue, his feet making almost no sound on the gritty road. The infrequent streetlamps made circles of orange light on the ground, with dark segments between them, like islands in a sea of blackness.

She's crazy to be wandering around alone at night, he thought. No wonder Mrs. Coutts is dithering with worry. If she has gone to Campbell's Bush our secret will be blown and her mother will never let her go again. That'll be the end of it. Stupid girl, what does she think she's doing?

It was so dark this evening that he overshot the spur line and almost missed the entrance to the passage. Walking along the ties in the dark was murder. He should have thought to bring a flashlight. He stumbled and recovered, remembering how Barbara had kidded him about his clumsiness the first time he'd come to Campbell's Bush.

He must be close to the fence now. There was no way of telling. He walked more cautiously, with his arms stretched out ahead of him. The darkness felt solid enough to touch. Then he stumbled over something that shouldn't — couldn't — be there. Something warm and soft. A muffled exclamation came from under him and before he had time to recover from his surprise he was being pummelled by two invisible fists.

He caught at the flailing arms — no easy matter in the

dark — and pinned them back. "Who are you?" he whispered fiercely.

"Terry. Terry Roberts. What do you think you're doing? You've got no business ... trespassers will be —"

"T-Terry? What on earth? Here, come away."

He dragged the smaller boy along the passage until they were back on 113th Avenue. In the streetlight Terry's face shone palely, his eyes looked red and sleepy. His mouth had fallen open and he looked like nothing so much as a surprised hamster.

"Stan, it can't be you! You ..."

Anger surged through Stan. "What in heck were you doing in there? How did you find out?"

"It's all right, Stan. I'll never tell. Never. I know it's your secret place. Yours and Barbara's. I wouldn't butt in or anything."

"But what were you *doing* there."

Terry muttered something inaudible. All Stan could catch was something about spies and being on guard.

"On guard? What on earth are you talking about?"

"Please don't laugh. It was the only thing I could do for you. To watch out and make sure that no one else came near your secret garden."

Stan felt unwilling laughter bubble up inside him as he looked down at the pink-eyed boy in his bulky windbreaker. "Okay, Terry. It's crazy, but I think I get it. But how come you didn't see me coming? Not much of a guard, are you?"

"I never fell asleep before, never. Honest, Stan. But I don't understand how you got over the fence without me hearing you."

"Over the fence? I didn't. I've just arrived."

"You can't have. I saw you inside. You and Barbara, cooking up something on your stove."

"I said I haven't been in the garden, you idiot. Not for a couple of days. Come on, own up. You didn't see a thing, did you, you short-sighted donkey?" He shook the smaller boy.

"I did. Honest. You were wearing your sweater. The one with the big bird knitted across the back. I'd know it anywhere. You're just kidding me, aren't you, Stan? You were there. You're just paying me back for watching you. But it wasn't like that, honestly. I was just keeping watch, like a good spy . . ."

"Oh, shut up snivelling, you idiot. I did *not* come over the fence. I haven't been here since Wednesday. If you saw two people, then there's someone else with Barbara."

"But nobody else knows, do they?"

"Unless she . . . but she wouldn't." Stan was suddenly fiercely sure of her. He shivered and dug his fists into his jacket pockets. There was a sick feeling in his stomach, like the day when he'd studied the wrong page for an exam and got every problem the wrong way round. Like the feeling he'd had when he'd seen Dad's grimy hands on his sketchbook.

Rage took over. Nobody was going to mess about with their special place. Nobody was going to scare or hurt Barbara. Only . . . why hadn't she yelled or run away when she saw someone there who wasn't him? On the verge of running down the passage and hurtling over the fence with doubled fists, he had a second thought. His rage chilled with caution. He grabbed Terry's arm.

"Back we go. Quietly. Got it?"

They could hear voices quite close by when they got

back to the fence. Barbara's and a man's. A strange voice. Every word was clear and separate on the still frosty air.

"Hold it steady. What's the matter with you?" The words were so close that Stan sank to his knees behind the fence, pulling Terry down with him. The voice had an edge of hysteria in it that sent a shiver down his back.

He peered through the crack. He could see a line of blue flame-points flickering on the Coleman stove. But the lean-to was empty. Where were they? He almost stood up and yelled, "Barbara, come out of there and stop being such an idiot!"

But something held him back. He heard the rustle of dry grass and the sound of cloth against cloth. The feeling of fear was so strong that it was like a fog closing in on him. He felt cold and his stomach heaved as if he were about to vomit.

There was a scratching noise and a sudden explosion of light. His eyes blinked automatically. When they opened again he saw Barbara's face lit by the flame of a match she was holding aloft. Her eyes looked enormous and shiny and, as he watched, she ran her tongue over her lips as if they were dry. The match went out and she quickly lit another. And another.

"Closer, can't you? I can't see what I'm doing."

The fourth match was held higher. For an instant the man's face was illuminated by the flame before he turned his back to the fence. A bland egg-shaped face, the forehead sloping up to a receding hairline of mousy hair. The eyes were set a little too close together, so they seemed to pinch the bridge of the very ordinary nose. A very ordinary face. Sort of like the image of the cornerstore owner.

Stan's own words echoed so clearly in his head that for a moment he was afraid he'd spoken them out loud. He suddenly knew that face. He had spent the evening studying the bones and muscles of it, sketching it, thinking about it.

He heard the blood rush through his veins, as loud as the ocean. Drumming in his ears. He felt icy cold and his head fell forward. I'm not going to faint, he told himself firmly. I couldn't be *that* stupid.

"Stan, what's the matter? Are you sick?"

Terry's voice was shrill in Stan's ears. The fog cleared and he was on his feet, his hand over Terry's mouth. He pointed down the passage and again they ran to the other end.

"What —" Terry's voice went up.

"Not here." Stan pulled him away from the entrance. "Voices carry like crazy in this cold. I mean, you could hear *them*, couldn't you?"

"You look awful, Stan."

"I'm f-fine." He took a deep breath and felt the frosty air burn the bottom of his lungs. "Listen, Terry, this is super important. You've got to run to Mrs. Coutts' house — it's in Westwood Acres —"

"I know the house."

"Right, then. Tell Mrs. Coutts that I've found Barbara and that she's in Campbell's — in this secret garden place. Tell her there's a man there. The man she gave me the photograph of. It's important, Terry. Make sure to tell her that. Tell her to get the police here right away. Got it?"

Terry nodded. "Are you going to tackle him, Stan? He's got a knife. I saw it glint. What are you going to —"

"I don't know. It depends. Get going now. Hurry!"

"Okay, Stan, you can count on me!"

Terry gasped out Stan's message to Mrs. Coutts and
waited after she had called the police. He would rather
have stayed with Stan and helped oust the intruder, but
'assisting the police in the execution of their duty' was
almost as good.

They arrived, their wide shoulders filling the tiny hall.
Mrs. Coutts got angrier and angrier. "I tell you it *is* Jack
Norton."

Terry hopped from foot to foot. "Stan'll be mad if you
don't get there soon. Why don't you hurry up?"

"That's enough from you, son. All right. Give me the
address."

"There isn't one. I'll have to show you."

"You can describe it, can't you?"

"Not really. It's secret. Really secret. You'd never
know."

In the end he was thrust into the back of the police car,
which he had counted on all the time he wasn't telling
them the address.

"They're saying Jack wasn't armed when he got away,"
one of the men remarked to the other.

"That's what Barbara called the man: Jack. Is he a
convict?" he asked breathlessly.

"Big-ears," muttered the driver under his breath. Then
he spoke over his shoulder to Terry. "Don't be scared,
sonny. We'll get your sister out safely."

"I'm *not* scared." His voice squeaked indignantly. "And
she's not my sister. She isn't even my friend."

"All right. Now pay attention. Where do we go?"

"It's on the left. A little way yet. Aren't you going to use
your siren?"

"We'd rather do it quietly with no fuss."

Terry blushed in the darkness. What a stupid mistake! Of course being quiet was important. "Over there," he shouted. "Stop!"

They pulled up close to the warehouse wall and got out. "Back there." Terry pointed. "Down that passage. Watch out for the ties."

"What ties?" The older policeman, the one who'd called him big-ears, turned, caught the tip of his shoe and nearly fell.

In the darkness Terry smiled. "Shall I lead the way?"

"No, you certainly won't. You stay right by the car, young man, and wait for our back-up. Show them where to go."

"Yes, sir."

"And don't budge."

"No, sir. You'd better hurry."

"Don't worry, son. Jack's not armed and he was never one for a gun anyway."

"He's got a knife now." Terry remembered seeing him carve something on the tree. How the knife had glittered in the flame. "He's nuts," he added.

"A knife? Norton has a knife?" The two men looked at each other and raced down the dark passage, leaving Terry pleased with the effect of his words.

"Got anything more to eat, girl?"

"I'll have a look." Barbara opened the cooler, wishing that it contained some miracle, like a tranquilizer gun or sleeping pills. But there was nothing in it but the almost empty tin of cocoa, a can of sardines and two chocolate bars.

"I hate sardines," Jack said passionately. "But you can hand over the chocolate."

He tore off the wrapping and crammed the squares into his mouth one after another, chomping and sucking, his mouth partly open, a dribble of chocolate escaping down his chin.

"That's good stuff," he said thickly. "Real good. You sure you got no more?"

"Sorry, nothing left but a spoonful or two of cocoa powder. Would you like me to make you some?"

"Can you do it without lumps? I hate lumpy cocoa."

"Of course. But there's no water. Where did you get the water for the soup, Jack?"

He chuckled. "From your stupid pond, of course. Once I'd got me feet wet I thought I'd put it to better use."

"I don't know how clean . . . but of course it's going to be boiled anyway." She stopped in confusion. How stupid to be worrying about germs, she thought, as she felt her way down to the pool with one of their mugs. I suppose if you're an escaped convict the last thing you'd be worrying about would be germs. She poured all but a bit of the water into the saucepan and set it on the stove. The rest she used to mix the cocoa powder to a paste in one of the mugs.

"So that's how it's done. I never knew that." He peered over her shoulder, watching her stir the paste smooth and pour the boiling water over it. It was a ridiculously domestic scene.

I am sitting here in the pitch dark showing a murderer how to make cocoa. Well, it's better than thinking: I am sitting in a place so secret no one will ever find me, with a murderer who has a knife.

She stirred the cocoa vigorously until it foamed.

"Ah, that's more like it!" He grabbed the mug from her hand.

132

Barbara shrank back into her corner of the lean-to, wishing she could really be invisible the way she used to pretend, back when she was just a kid. Please, God, get me out of here. I'll always do what Mom says and I'll keep my room clean and never complain. If only —

"You got the time?" Jack asked.

She jumped and then held her wrist close to the light of the stove. "Seven-fifty."

And pitch dark. Mom would be frantic. She'd said she was just going for a walk. Hours ago.

The moon shone suddenly through a rift in the cloud behind them. It made Campbell's Bush look like a garden from another planet, silver and grey and magical. If she were safely here with Stan it would be beautiful. Now it looked sinister.

"I've got to get some shut-eye before morning. Didn't get a wink last night. Once the streets are crowded in the morning I'll be off. No one'll notice me in a crowd. And I've got friends. Oh, yes, I've still got friends. In the morning I'll be okay. But right now I've got to get some sleep." He turned his smooth face, shining in the moonlight, towards Barbara. "So what the hell am I going to do with you?"

It was the moment she had dreaded, the moment she had put off as long as possible with conversation, with food and drink, with friendliness. But it had come anyway. The moment when Jack realized that she really *was* the enemy. That she was in his way. She wondered if he could hear her heartbeats in the silence.

His eyes shifted, alternately bright and dark as they caught the moonlight. They shone like the knife blade. The silence was unbearable.

"Why don't I go and leave you in peace? I'll promise not

to tell. Or I could stay and keep watch while you have a good sleep. Would you like that?" Her voice faded. She felt ashamed. He was a murderer and she was pleading with him, offering to *help* him.

"Are you wearing those nylon things?" It was a totally unexpected question, as was the hand that came down heavily on her leg.

She flinched and swallowed a scream. "Wh-what?"

"Don't be stupid. Plain English, isn't it? What d'you call them? Pantyhose."

"Yes. Yes, I am."

"Take 'em off, then."

Barbara's courage snapped. She could hear herself screaming "I won't, I won't," knowing as she screamed that it was the worst thing she could do, but not being able to stop.

He was on his knees beside her, shaking her so hard that her teeth rattled. "Shut up. I don't mean anything bad. Shut up!"

She couldn't stop. He pulled her to her feet, clamped a hand over her mouth. She beat against his chest, trying to pull away. His hand smelled of sweat and dirt.

"Don't make that noise. Please don't. That's what *they* did. My mom and *him*. Don't make me do it again."

With an enormous effort Barbara managed to stop screaming. She could feel the fear boiling inside her, forcing itself up through her throat in a horrible whining sound, the sound of a trapped rabbit. Jack Norton's rabbit.

"I just want your nylons to tie you up. So you won't run off when I'm asleep and bring the cops. I won't hurt you. I promise. Please don't make me mad."

At Barbara's first scream Stan leapt over the fence. It was a perfect vault, one that Barbara would have been proud of, one that Mrs. Rawlings wouldn't have believed even if she'd seen it. He landed neatly on the balls of his feet and sprinted silently across to the south wall, the only part of the garden not lit by the intrusive moon. He crept along in the shadows, finishing up in a crouch close to the lean-to.

Norton was bent over directly in front of him, his back towards Stan. He could see the knife in the man's hand, its blade glinting wickedly in the moonlight. He couldn't see Barbara at all. He didn't know why she had screamed, nor what had silenced her. For a second he had the sickening feeling that he was too late, that it was all over, but, as his stomach knotted and lurched, she screamed again in the darkness.

"I won't, I won't!"

The black shape that was Jack Norton's back altered, became taller and thinner. He was standing now, only a couple of metres from where Stan crouched in the shadow of the wall. He moved to one side and now Stan could see Barbara's face past the darkness of Norton's shoulder. It was white in the moonlight. Her eyes were shut and her mouth was open in a black *O*. She wasn't screaming anymore, but the silence in the garden was so profound that Stan could hear, beyond Norton's harsh breathing, a stifled whine. It reminded him of an animal in a trap. In a moment she would scream again, he knew.

Norton had Barbara's arms pinned behind her, and now Stan saw that one hand had come up to cover her mouth. One hand holding down her arms, one over her mouth. Two hands, no knife. Stan felt a small surge of hope, and he crept cautiously forward on hands and knees, feeling through the long grass. His hands fumbled frantically. He was almost at Norton's feet now. He could feel them shift as the man struggled with Barbara. Where was the moonlight when he so desperately needed it?

He glanced over his shoulder. A small milky thread of cloud. Nothing really. Only it made the difference between life and death. At last the moon slid free, white light poured down on the dark glade, and the knife shone like a silver thread in the long grass. He reached forward and grasped its handle. The wind stirred the grass and chilled the sweat on his face. Perhaps twenty seconds had gone by. It had felt like a lifetime.

He rose to his feet, gripping the knife until his knuckles were white, and yelled "Let her go!" His voice came out high, like a little kid's. He swallowed and yelled again. Norton turned, holding Barbara in front of him as a shield between him and Stan.

"Stan!"

"It's okay, Barbara. Don't be scared. I've got the knife. Let her go, you!"

"Not likely, sonny. She's going to get me out of here, aren't you, B.C.?"

"I've got the knife. I'll . . ."

"You'll do what? Stick it between my ribs? Go pare your toenails with it, sonny. You're out of your league." As he spoke Norton began to back slowly towards the fence, keeping Barbara in front of him.

Some distraction, thought Stan, just so I can run for the fence and get over it before he does. His frantic eyes caught the small flames of the stove and, without giving himself time to think of the consequences, his toe reached out and kicked it over.

He heard Norton's curse and Barbara's muffled shriek in almost the same instant that the flames caught. It was like a slow-motion explosion, flames running through the grass, and then a sudden golden light blotting out the pale moon. The heat on his face and bare hands was unbearable. For an instant he was back in the yard at home, snatching his sketchbook from the incinerator, feeling the agonizing pain of his burns.

He fought his paralyzing fear and leapt the flames. Now he stood between Norton and the fence. His back was to the fence, the slats digging into his shoulders. Norton had whirled around, with Barbara struggling in his arms, screaming.

"D'you want us all to burn?" Stan yelled. "It's no good, Norton. Let her go."

Norton didn't move. And in Stan's ears, as he wondered desperately what to do next, was a quiet and comforting whisper. "All right, son. Just move over to your left, away from the fence."

He obeyed without taking his eyes off Barbara and Norton, silhouetted against the flaming grass. His heart thudded.

The fence crashed to the ground and the little garden was suddenly full of men. Men struggling, men splashing water from the pool, stamping out the flames. Someone took the knife from Stan's hand and he found he was next to Barbara, his arms holding her tight.

"You okay?"

"Yes. Yes, I think so. Oh, Stan!" They silently watched the policemen take Jack Norton away. He seemed to have shrunk, thought Barbara. He wasn't much taller than she was, and much of his bulk was Stan's sweater.

"I wouldn't have hurt you, miss," he said over and over,

as they hauled him through the debris of the fence. "I just wanted your nylons to tie you up so I could sleep. I wouldn't have hurt her," he said to the policeman. "She makes great cocoa. No lumps in it. Mom's cocoa always had lumps. Old cow."

"That's okay then, Jack. Put your hands together. That's it."

Barbara and Stan heard the final click of handcuffs. Then they all trampled over the fallen fence and down the passage. She stopped and looked back. The last officer had stamped out the remaining sparks and now pulled up the plastic liner of the pool, tipping the rest of the water over the mess. His flashlight wavered over their secret garden, over trampled grass, soot and wetness.

She turned away and followed Stan and the others down the passage to 113th Avenue, to be put into a car and driven home. Mom was waiting at the door and she ran into her arms as she hadn't done since she was a little kid.

Terry strolled out of the shadows as soon as he saw Barbara stowed in a car and driven away. He looked up at Stan and Stan looked down at him, seeing the gleam in his eyes, glimpsing the would-be spy.

"Thanks, Terry. We couldn't have managed without you."

Then they were driven home. At the Natyshyn house Stan's mom was hovering by the door. "Stan, I've been so worried. I was going to call the police, but your father wouldn't let me. Are you all right? What happened? Your jacket! It's covered with soot and—"

"Stop babying the boy, Mother. Where the heck have you been, Stan?"

"I'll tell you about it in the morning. Right now I'm just too bushed."

He headed upstairs without even noticing the astonished faces in the living room. It wasn't until he was brushing his teeth that he realized he'd talked back to his dad without stammering once.

Winter came, and the first snow. Barbara imagined all the horror of trampled grass and mud and soot in the secret garden all covered over with the clean whiteness of snow, and she felt better. Christmas came, and then the holidays. When school started again she had a long serious talk with Mrs. Rawlings, who agreed to take her back on the gym team once she was in Grade Eight.

Spring came reluctantly. The snow shrank away, leaving behind drifts of sandy dirt, lost overshoes and orphaned mitts. The ground thawed and the first tulips began to appear in front yards.

One day Barbara saw a robin strutting across the lawn, and she couldn't help wondering whether the grass had grown up over the burnt patch in Campbell's Bush. Would the purple martins decide to take up residence in their new apartment house? And for how long would the garden continue to flourish before the Hong Kong project took over the industrial park. If indeed it did. She longed to know. But she had promised Mom that she would never go back.

Luckily Stan's family had bound him with no such promises. One sunny day in early May he walked along 113th Avenue. He turned into the secret passage and was brought up short by a chain-link fence, higher than his upstretched arm, with a nasty-looking line of barbed wire along the top and a notice saying that the City would Prosecute Trespassers.

Barbara's face fell when he told her what had happened. "It's like a door shutting forever on a beautiful dream. I wish now I'd never asked you to look."

"Hang on, Barb, I haven't finished. Down in the left-hand corner, right against the wall, something has scrabbled a kind of tunnel under the wire."

"Some*thing*?"

"I reckon the hole would be just big enough for a jackrabbit."

Their jackrabbit! He'd been the beginning of the adventure, leading her down the passageway to discovery. He'd been her link with Stan. And here he was, still finding his way to the secret garden, in spite of all the city could do.

Even if Campbell's Bush *was* bulldozed, Barbara realized, the jackrabbit would find another place to be alone. Probably there were dozens of small secret gardens, little pockets of leftover countryside, hidden in the city, waiting for the jackrabbit to find refuge in them. And other children too.

Her eyes lit up. "So that's all right, then."